"Don't move."

Jace took advantage of the moment to withdraw his sidearm and press the barrel to the guy's skull.

Malice radiated from the dark as coal eyes stared back at Jace.

Jace's gaze searched for Abby and found her already with the phone in her hand. Her wide, shocked eyes were on him as she spoke to the 911 dispatcher.

"Wyatt? Who are you?"

Jace gritted his teeth. "Not now."

He couldn't let this thug know his true identity or his true purpose for being in Washington state for fear the goon would report back to the Garcia Cartel that Abby was under the protection of the US marshal's service. But the way Abby's eyes narrowed and her delicate jaw firmed with obvious anger despite the purple mark forming on her cheek, told Jace in no uncertain terms a moment of reckoning was coming.

But unfortunately, he wouldn't be able to give her the answers she wanted or deserved. Not if he was to stay true to his mission, which was to keep her safe. And in the dark.

Terri Reed's romance and romantic suspense novels have appeared on the *Publishers Weekly* top twenty-five and NPD BookScan top one hundred lists and have been featured in *USA TODAY, Christian Fiction* magazine and *RT Book Reviews.* Her books have been finalists for the Romance Writers of America RITA® Award and the National Readers' Choice Award and finalists three times for the American Christian Fiction Writers Carol Award. Contact Terri at terrireed.com or PO Box 19555, Portland, OR 97224.

Fear thou not; for I am with thee: be not dismayed;
for I am thy God: I will strengthen thee;
yea, I will help thee; yea, I will uphold thee
with the right hand of my righteousness.
—*Isaiah* 41:10

To my husband.
I am so grateful we are doing life together.

ONE

The cold October night shimmered with rain as the last of the employee vehicles left the parking lot. A shiver of unease slid over Abby Frost.

Mentally checking off the list of closing tasks associated with her job as the assistant branch manager of the Pacific Northwest Savings and Loan in Camas, Washington, she assured herself she'd followed all the proper procedures. The vault was locked up tight, the bank security system engaged and the doors armed.

There was no reason for the creeping anxiety dogging her steps as she hurried toward where she'd parked.

Something wasn't right. Her steps faltered as her eyes adjusted to the inky shadows.

The parking lot was too dark.

Why were the overhead lights not providing the warm glow of security?

She always parked under one of the lights as a safety precaution. She made a mental note to call the electric company to service the parking lot lights. A responsibility she didn't mind taking on.

Hitching the strap of her cross-body purse higher on her shoulder, she flipped up the hood of her waterproof coat. The rain the Pacific Northwest was famous for had her doubling her pace across the lot toward her small SUV. Shelter and safety waited, like an old friend.

A car on the street beyond the parking lot drove by; the bright headlights washed over her, exposing her and making her wince against the glare.

The crunch of glass beneath her low heels made the hairs at the back of her neck rise in alarm. The overhead light wasn't on the fritz. Someone had deliberately broken the light bulbs near her vehicle.

A chill having nothing to do with the weather skated down her spine.

She glanced around and noticed a sedan she didn't recognize parked at the back of the lot. It appeared empty. Abandoned? Another issue she'd need to deal with in the morning.

Her hands shook as much from the cold seeping into her bones as from the crawling sensation of being watched. She fumbled with the key fob and hit the button to unlock her car. The interior lights came on when the unlock mechanism engaged. A welcoming sight.

As she reached for the door handle, the sound of a rush of footsteps punched her heart into her throat. There was no time for self-preservation before rough hands grabbed her, and she let out a startled yelp. The assailant dragged her backward toward the sedan, her heels scraping on the blacktop.

Please, God, no!

All her nerve endings fired, as if an exposed electric wire touched her skin. For a heartbeat, she seized, completely at a loss of what to do. Then the rapid drops of rain pelting her and her attacker jolted her out of the rising panic. The self-defense class tactics she'd taken last summer with her best friend, Lisa, reared to the forefront of her consciousness.

The instructor's words echoed in her head. *If you're ever attacked from behind, go limp. Then fight back. Do everything you can to get away. Don't make it easy for your assailant. Use...*

Pepper spray.

In the side pocket of her purse.

She groped for the small canister. Once her fingers wrapped around the metal tube, she positioned her thumb over the release valve. Barely able to draw a breath past the arms tightly squeezing her chest, she went limp.

The man holding her cursed into her right ear and stumbled as he took her full weight. Not waiting for him to recover from his surprise, because, really, she doubted her hundred and thirty pounds were too much for him, she lifted the pepper container and let loose a stream of oleoresin capsicum gel over her right shoulder and prayed her aim was true. Unlike a spray that could blow back into her face, the thick burning substance would stick to her attacker's skin and give her time to escape.

The assailant let out a yowl of pain and released his hold on her. She crumpled to the ground, and the grit and broken glass littering the parking lot dug into her knees and hands.

Get away, get away.

The mantra echoed through her head, galvanizing her into action. She scrambled to her feet and ran back to the bank building, while digging her keys from within her purse. With shaky hands, she unlocked and yanked open the bank door, then stepped inside. After securing the door closed, she turned the lock. Within seconds, the bank security alarm triggered, a shrill noise filling the air while also sending an alert to the local police department. Help was on the way.

Through the glass of the bank door, she watched her attacker jump into his sedan and peel out of the lot. She sagged in relief.

What had just happened? Why would someone attack her? Was it random? Or had she been targeted?

Three hours later, after giving her statement to the police and going through all the rigmarole created by a breach in bank security, Abby was in her SUV and headed to her apartment, empty save for her cat, Daisy. She sent up a prayer for safety, suddenly regretting she didn't have anyone special to call.

Unfortunately, she wasn't dating anyone and hadn't in a long time. She didn't have any objections to romance. She secretly longed for her one true love. But too many things could go wrong, like they had with

Brad Stone in high school. If she gave her heart and it wasn't enough, if she wasn't enough... How could she handle heartbreak again?

Better not to try than to risk rejection.

She turned the heat up, but even the warm air blowing out of the vents couldn't stop the shivers racking her body.

Was she being followed?

Her gaze strayed to the rearview mirror. There were too many cars out for her peace of mind. She circled her block twice before finally slipping into her parking space and turning off the motor. She sat with her cell phone in her hand, poised to hit the button for 911, and waited.

After a long moment of nothing happening but her own anxiety creeping upward, she forced herself to hurry from her car to her apartment building door. Her electronic key fob unlocked the entrance, and she hustled inside, then made sure the door closed completely behind her. Then she took the stairs two at a time, her heels clacking on the tile, to her third-floor apartment.

Once inside with the door securely locked, she released a breath and sank onto her couch. Daisy jumped onto her lap and rubbed her head against Abby's chest. Burying her face into the Himalayan's white-and-black fur, Abby finally let out a sob.

She'd never been so scared in her life. And she hoped never to be again. She sent praises Heavenward for arriving home safely.

The trill of her cell phone made her jump. Abby set Daisy down and hurried to the kitchen counter to fish her phone out of her purse. The bank branch manager's name came up on the caller identification screen.

Abby pressed the answer button. "Hello."

"Are you okay?" Paul Morgan asked. "I shouldn't have left early tonight."

"You have a sick kid at home, and Teresa had to get to work." His wife was a critical-care nurse at the hospital. "I'm fine now," she assured him and herself. "You couldn't have known. And the guy could have just as easily tried to mug you."

Though a tiny voice in her head whispered the man wasn't a mugger. He'd intended to abduct her. Another chill skated over her skin.

Paul let out a breath, and she could picture him pinching the bridge of his nose beneath his black-rimmed glasses.

"I'm really glad you're okay, Abby. Take the rest of the week off."

She had so much already piled up on her desk. Taking time off would put her behind, and then she'd have to put in overtime to catch up. "I don't—" she protested.

"I insist. Actually, corporate insists. With pay."

He'd discussed her with corporate?

She had her eye on managing her own branch. Would this incident make her appear weak and incapable, and therefore put her out of the running for moving up? "I appreciate the offer, but I'm fine. I need to work. I can't just do nothing."

"You won't be doing nothing." Paul's voice gentled. "You'll be recovering."

He made it sound like she'd had surgery. She gritted her teeth. "I've recovered."

"You've been through a shock."

Understatement.

"There's no shame in taking time off."

Her gut twisted. But who would do her job while she was gone? "I don't want—"

"Abby, *I* don't want you to come in until next week. Understood?"

She slumped back onto the couch. "If I must."

"Yes, you must."

She thanked him for his concern and said goodbye. "Well, Daisy, we've got a few days of downtime."

The cat meowed in answer, bringing a smile to Abby. "At least you need me." Daisy let out another yowl. "Right. You're hungry. One of the reasons you love me. I'm your food source."

After feeding Daisy, Abby took a long, hot shower and changed into warm sweats. When she emerged from her bedroom, she checked her phone and noted a missed call from her younger sister, Nancy.

Snuggling under a blanket on the couch, Abby hit the button to call her sister.

"Hey," Nancy answered. "Are you home?"

"Yes, I'm home. But it's been a harrowing evening." Abby told her sister about being assaulted at the bank.

"Wow, scary." Nancy's voice rose several octaves. "Do you want me to come over?"

Warmth spread through Abby's chest. She was home now and safe. She was fine. But she wasn't up for the whirlwind of her extroverted, exuberant sister's energy. They were as different as siblings could be. Nancy had red hair, fair skin and freckles, while Abby's skin tanned easily; her honey-blond hair darkened in the winter and lightened in the summer. They both had hazel eyes, only Nancy's were more green than gold like Abby's.

"I love you for offering, but not tonight," Abby said, hoping the rebuff wouldn't hurt Nancy. "I'm taking a few days off, so maybe later this week."

"Good! Though I'm not happy it took you being mugged to finally take a vacation."

It was tempting to let her sister believe taking time away from work had been Abby's idea. "It's a forced leave. We'll get together soon, I promise."

"Okay, if you're sure." The doubt in Nancy's voice was sweet and filled Abby with affection. "Uh, I called to tell you to check your inbox. The results of our DNA test on the genealogy site came back. I connected you to my results. But you made yours private. You don't have to do it tonight."

Abby had forgotten they'd done the test. "I will open it later, thanks. Love you, sis."

"Love you, too." Nancy hung up.

For a long moment, Abby sat unmoving on the couch. The attack played on a loop through her mind, making her shudder.

A cold finger of fear whispered across her neck. Why had the stranger grabbed her?

She didn't want to contemplate what

he'd intended. However, her active imagination wouldn't cooperate. She'd watched too many reality news shows and crime dramas. People went missing all the time. Some never to be heard from again.

Argh! She rose, paced the living room and then moved to the kitchen. Keeping her hands busy helped to calm her. She made herself a turkey sandwich and grabbed her laptop from the kitchen counter. Sitting at the round dining table, she ate while she fired up the computer.

Needing a distraction, she opened the email from the genealogy site. The results popped up. She clicked through the site to connect to her sister. A comparison between her and her sister's DNA profiles filled the screen.

A knot formed in Abby's chest. She didn't understand what she was reading. Though she and Nancy shared many DNA markers, Abby had several not connected to her sister. All of them on their paternal side. Confusion and a sick sort of dread balled in her chest. She clicked on the DNA relatives tab and found she connected to a family by the name of Ramirez-Estevan. But her sister didn't.

Heart beating like a bird trapped in a cage, Abby jumped to her feet and paced as the realization formed. The only plausible explanation was the man who'd raised Abby, the one she'd called dad until his death two years earlier, wasn't her father.

This couldn't be true.

She grabbed her phone and dialed her mother's number. When her mom answered, Abby blurted, "Was Dad my dad? I mean, my biological father?"

Silence met her questions.

A sinking stone of hurt landed in Abby's gut. "Mom?"

"Oh, Abby," her mom said. "I'm sorry I've kept this from you."

Abby sank to the floor. Her world crumbled. "Tell me everything."

The metallic ring of the desk phone gave deputy US marshal Jace Armstrong the perfect excuse not to answer his father's question of whether he was bringing a date to the family ranch for dinner this weekend. He had no intention of riding the dating carousel again.

Each of his relationships had ended the same, with him bowing out before things became too serious. Growing up with a dad who was gone for long periods of time with no communication had left a scar and made Jace leery of committing.

No way would he inflict the pain of loneliness and uncertainty he and his mom had had to deal with on anyone else. But he kept the truth all to himself. No reason to lay a guilt trip on his dad for doing his job, a job that saved lives and kept the country safe. A job Jace now embraced.

As his father leaned forward to press the intercom button connecting him to his long-term admin, Jace witnessed his dad turn from nosy parent to his boss, US marshal of the western district of Texas. "Yes, Regina?"

"There's a woman on the line who'd like to speak to Deputy Marshal Armstrong regarding a man named Carlos Reyes. Should I put her through?"

Gavin Armstrong's ruddy complexion turned ashen.

Jace leaned forward with concern. "Dad?"

Giving his head a shake as if coming out of a shock, Gavin said, "Yes. I'll take the call."

"Line one," Regina said and clicked off.

Gavin punched the button on the multiline phone. "Who am I speaking with?"

Jace's eyebrows rose. His father was keeping the call on Speaker. Curious?

"Hello, my name is Abigail Frost." The female voice was melodic and soft. "Are you deputy US marshal Gavin Armstrong?"

"I am." Gavin's tone held a note of wariness. "What can I help you with?"

Jace tucked in his chin. His father hadn't been a deputy in more than a decade. This obviously had something to do with an old case.

"I need to know what you can tell me about Carlos Reyes," the woman said.

"How did you get this number?" Gavin asked. "And why would I know anything about this man?"

"My mother, Mandy Urquhart-Frost, gave me a business card you left with her thirty years ago when you came to inform her of Carlos Reyes's death."

"That was a long time ago," Gavin said. "Why are you asking now?"

"Yes, of course, forgive me," Abigail said. "Carlos Reyes was my biological father. I only recently learned of this."

Gavin sat back, clearly stunned. He ran a hand through his still-thick salt-and-pepper hair.

Jace rose, concerned his father was having another heart attack.

Recovering, Gavin waved him off. "I didn't know about you. I'm sorry—I don't have any more information to give other than what I told your mother."

"Do you happen to know if Carlos Reyes had siblings?"

"I couldn't really say," Gavin commented. "Why?"

"I did a DNA test and am connected to a family by the name of Ramirez-Estevan. I'm assuming it has to be through either a sister or maybe a cousin of Carlos Reyes."

A deep frown marred Gavin's forehead. "Mrs. Frost—"

"Miss, actually," Abigail said.

"Miss Frost." Gavin's voice dropped in pitch. There was no mistaking the grave seriousness of his tone. Jace stared at his father, noting the tension in his posture. He was clearly distressed. "I would caution you against making contact with this family. Whatever genetic connection you have may only stir up old wounds if true."

There was a moment of silence. Then Abigail said, "Can you tell me how Carlos died?"

"No, I can't," Gavin said. "I would suggest you forget you ever heard the name Carlos Reyes."

"What aren't you saying?" The woman's voice held a brisk note.

Jace wanted to know the answer, as well.

"There is nothing more I can tell you," Gavin said. "Good day, Miss Frost."

He disconnected the call, scrubbed a hand down his face and then pinned Jace with an intense stare. "I have a very classified assignment for you. You need to find this Abigail Frost and keep her safe."

A twitch of unease made Jace restless. "What's going on?"

"Shut the door."

Once the door was closed, Gavin said, "Carlos Reyes was a witness to a murder perpetrated by the son of the head of one of the country's most ruthless drug cartels. Carlos was set to testify, but someone leaked his location from within the department."

"A mole?" Acid churned in Jace's gut. "Within the marshals service?"

His father rested his elbows on the desk and steepled his hands. "I never found the leak in either the marshals service or in the Justice Department. But I know there was one."

Dreading the answer, Jace had to ask, "He was your witness?"

His father gave a slow nod.

"What happened to him?"

Gavin placed his hands flat on the desk. "Carlos disappeared."

Surprise arced through Jace. "So he's not dead?"

"Not as far as I know."

"Why tell Miss Frost's mother he was?"

"Before Carlos would agree to testify, he made me promise to tell the woman he was leaving behind he was dead. He didn't want her searching for him. He didn't want her in danger."

"Thoughtful of him. But why didn't he go through with his testimony?"

"Fear. The cartel has a long reach. I threatened, cajoled and pleaded, but Carlos refused to testify and declined going into WITSEC. I didn't blame him for being reluctant. We were compromised. He went completely off the grid. I lost touch with him about ten years ago." Regret, and some other emotion Jace couldn't quite place, laced his words. "And now his daughter could be in danger. If Tomas Garcia, the head of the Garcia Cartel, learns about her, they could use her to draw out Carlos."

After three days holed up in her apartment alternating between tears of hurt and outrage, Abby stopped crying.

Everything since Tuesday night seemed surreal. As if the assault hadn't been traumatic enough, learning her dad wasn't her biological father and hearing her mother sob as she told Abby about her first love and his death had left Abby adrift. The strange call to the US marshal had been less than helpful. The man had clearly been hiding something.

So many questions floated around in her head. Why had Carlos Reyes been involved with the marshals service? Was he a witness? A fugitive? Or had he worked for the government? Why had someone attempted to kidnap her? Would the assailant strike again?

Realizing her parents had lied her whole life was the most devastating blow. How could she ever trust her mother again?

How could she trust anyone?

Tired of the spinning wheel of her own thoughts, she focused on her responsibilities. Namely Daisy. She'd fed the cat the last of her food this morning. Abby really needed to go grocery shopping for herself, as well.

The idea of leaving the safety of the apartment triggered a nervous churning in her stomach. She contemplated asking her mom, Nancy or Lisa to go to the store for her. Or she could have her groceries delivered. But she didn't want to wait.

Forcing herself off the couch, she straightened her spine. She wasn't going to let fear keep her a prisoner in her apartment. If she did, she'd never leave. An unacceptable prospect. She had a life to live, a job she enjoyed and friends who needed her.

The trip to the market had her nerves stretched to the point of snapping. Normally, she enjoyed shopping, but today she sped through her grocery list like a pack of wolves was hot on her heels. She couldn't get home fast enough. She parked in her designated spot outside her apartment building, breathing hard. Her heart pounded, and her head throbbed from the stress.

Maybe she should seek counseling. Her church had people available to talk to.

Thankfully, the autumn daylight had chased away the past few days of rain. Muted sunlight, filtered by the cloud cover, bathed the world in shades of gray. Nothing helped ease the residual fears from the trauma of being attacked or the ache of being lied to.

Stepping from her vehicle, she glanced around, searching for a threat. Her gaze snagged on a gold sedan she didn't recognize a few spaces away. Had the sedan the other night been gold? She couldn't recall. Her heart rate ticked up. She was being silly. A silver truck pulled into the lot and parked across the way, but the driver, hidden behind tinted windows, didn't get out.

Moving quickly, she popped the trunk of her SUV and grabbed her grocery bags. She needed to get inside, where she'd be safe. When she turned around, a man stood directly in front of her.

She let out a gasp of fright.

His dark hair was sheared short, and he had red-rimmed eyes filled with malice in their inky depths.

Reacting to a sudden surge of adrenaline, she dropped the grocery bags. Their contents spilled on the ground at her feet. She jammed her hand into the outside pocket of her purse, curling her fingers over the pepper gel container.

The man's hand shot out and grasped her wrist, twisting her hand until she dropped the canister and yelped in pain. "Not this time, princess."

He yanked her to him, snaking his arm around her middle in a tight grip, and dragged her toward the gold sedan.

Chest tight with fear, she thrashed, kicking at his legs, clawing at his arms and screaming at the top of her lungs.

Then, suddenly, she was loose.

Her assailant was taken to the ground and put flat on his stomach by a cowboy. A real-life, hat-toting, boot-wearing cowboy. A lightweight raincoat stretched over broad shoulders as he held the attacker's hands together in a strong grip. He reached into the back pocket of his well-worn jeans and produced a white plastic zip tie to secure the man's wrists together.

"Call 911." The cowboy's voice had a pleasing authentic drawl. Warm brown eyes the color of her favorite chocolate treat locked on her. "It's okay. He's not going to hurt you now. I promise."

She scooped up the pepper gel canister. For some reason, Abby wanted to believe him, but did she dare trust him?

TWO

Jace yanked the goon who'd tried to kidnap Abigail to his feet. He wanted to question the guy, demand to know if he was acting on behalf of the Garcia Cartel. But Jace couldn't risk blowing his cover. Letting his true identity slip could put Abigail in danger, not to mention put his own family and friends in jeopardy.

His gaze zeroed in on Abigail Frost. Her DMV photo didn't do her justice. Nor hint at her feisty spirit.

There was nothing at all frosty about the woman. Shoulder-length honey-blond hair framed an oval face with a smattering of freckles over the bridge of her straight nose. Her well-shaped mouth was pressed into a thin line. She stared at Jace with wide hazel eyes, the pupils dilated, and the personal defense product held to her chest like a shield. He recognized the signs. Shock. And a good dose of fear.

Jace raised an eyebrow and gently prompted, "911?"

Abigail bobbed her head in agreement and scurried to where her purse lay on the ground surrounded by the scattered groceries. Despite the loose-fitting outfit, there was no mistaking the woman's curves.

The assailant tried to twist away from Jace's grasp.

Heart still pumping with adrenaline, Jace yanked his gaze from the pretty blonde and tightened his hold on the thug's biceps. The man wore a black rain slicker over a navy hoodie jacket and chino pants. "Hold still."

A stab of remorse had Jace's lip curling. He should have acted quicker. He'd seen the man a half second before he stepped out of the bushes and made a grab for Abi-

gail. Jace had been too far away to inter-
vene before the creep put his hands on her.

His only excuse was fatigue. He'd spent
the past forty-eight hours making arrangements to get to the Pacific Northwest,
which included convincing the tenant in
the apartment across from Abigail in her
building to take an extended overseas assignment for his company. It had taken a
bit of finagling to pressure the man's em-
ployer into complying. But the sway of the
US Marshals Service couldn't be denied.

Miss Frost hadn't left her apartment
until this afternoon. Jace had trailed her to
the supermarket, where she'd made a mad
dash down each aisle with her shopping
cart like she was a contestant on one of
those grocery game shows. Jace had made
himself invisible, keeping a good distance from the woman while still keeping
eyes on her. He'd hung back once they'd
reached the apartment complex, simply to
let her get to her things and head inside
before he followed her into the building.

He'd let down his guard.

A blunder nearly costing Abigail Frost her life.

He wouldn't be so careless again. Surveil and protect.

However, from now on, he would be sticking closer, making this personal. He vowed not to let anyone hurt her. The drive to succeed, to be the best, spurred his conscience like a bronc rider in the rodeo. He couldn't let his father down. Nor could he let the cartel win. Getting close to his charge was the best way to keep her safe. Befriending her and inserting himself into her life would ensure he had access to properly protect and defend against anything the cartel tried to do.

Rescuing her from the clutches of the would-be kidnapper should give Jace a way into Abigail's circle of trust. An "in" he would use to his advantage.

Within minutes, shrill police sirens filled the air. Jace didn't doubt his alias would hold up to any scrutiny, but keeping the locals in the dark regarding the danger threatening their community didn't sit well.

But to keep Abigail Frost safe, he'd stick to the role he was playing—helpful newcomer to the picturesque town of Camas, Washington. His undercover name of Wyatt Prescott would ensure there was no connection to the Armstrong family. A necessary precaution to protect those he loved.

Two cruisers came to a halt nearby. Officers climbed out of the nearest vehicle and approached with hands on their weapons.

Abigail hurried to the closest officer, a rush of words spilling out of her mouth like water from a faucet as she explained the situation. She did a pretty good job of it. Jace was impressed. No hysterics, no tears. Just the facts.

Two other officers moved to Jace's side.

"We'll take it from here," the older of the two said.

With a nod, Jace relinquished the suspect to the officer's custody.

"Sir," another officer said. "We need to take your statement."

"Of course." Jace moved away from where Abigail was now giving a more detailed statement to the lawman.

Familiar with the drill, Jace told the officer in concise words how he'd happened upon the lady being manhandled by the attacker. "It was clear she didn't know him or want his attention."

Jace was careful not to reveal his suspicions regarding the offender's intent to kidnap her or the likelihood he worked for the Garcia Cartel. The local police would have to do their own investigating. Jace wasn't here to bust some hired muscle. He was here to protect a woman in jeopardy.

Once the police's questions had been answered and the suspect driven away, Jace turned to Abigail. She stood frozen in place with her purse over her shoulder, one hand in the outside pocket and the other hand fisted at her side. She stared at the ground littered with her dry goods, fruits and veggies, and cans of cat food.

Afraid to move too fast and cause her to bolt like a skittish colt, Jace slowly began to pick up her groceries and put them back into the recycled material bags scattered on the ground.

With a sound of clear dismay, Abigail darted forward and scooped up the cans of cat food. "You don't have to help. You've already saved my life. I can deal with this."

"Now, what kind of gentleman would I be if I didn't offer my services to a damsel in distress?" Jace said with a grin.

She blinked at him, the colors in her hazel eyes shifting between gold and green. "Are you for real?"

Jace chuckled and touched the brim of his hat. "Yes, ma'am."

The shape of a V appeared between her dark blond eyebrows. "Did you just *ma'am* me?"

"Is that not allowed here in the Pacific Northwest?" Color had returned to her complexion and a rosy hue now highlighted her angular cheekbones. So pretty.

And not to mention reassuring. She had clearly regained her composure.

She turned away, but not before he glimpsed the spark of humor in her eyes. "It's allowed. Just unusual here. Pacific Northwesterners aren't terribly formal. Most are a bit bohemian."

"Good to know." He'd pictured lumber-jacks and tree huggers rather than bohe-mian types.

"Why did you have zip ties in your pocket?"

The question had him grimacing, and he was thankful she wasn't watching him. "Doesn't every man have zip ties in their pocket?"

His jesting earned him her focus and another frown. "If they are a criminal."

Good point. "No, seriously. I'm in the process of moving and had some left over." Needing to redirect the conversation, he picked up a tub of ice cream. "Mmm. My favorite."

She glanced at what he held and then her

gaze met his with another spark of humor. "Who doesn't love rocky road?"

"Exactly. It has it all. Sweet marshmallows, chocolate and crunchy nuts." He put the ice cream in the bag. "Oops, a stray apple." He shimmied beneath her small SUV and grabbed the delicious red fruit.

When he stood, he offered it to her. She eyed the apple as if it might be poisoned. Finally, she held out her hand. He set the apple on her outstretched palm. An offering of sorts.

"Thank you for your heroics." She tucked the apple into her bag.

A strange sort of restlessness tightened the muscles of his shoulders. "I'm no hero."

"You are to me." She moved to pick up the second bag, the one he'd packed.

"I'll get it." He beat her to the bag.

She seemed at a loss. Her gaze went from him to the door of the apartment building and back. Clearly, caution was keeping her from inviting him in. Taking pity on her, he said, "I'm renting apartment 3D."

Her eyes flared and then narrowed. "What happened to Mack?"

Jace shrugged. "A work thing. I'm subletting until he returns."

"Oh. I didn't know."

They walked to the building. She stepped aside to allow him to use the electronic key fob to open the entrance door. Smart move on her part, making him prove he had access to the building. He liked this woman.

When they made it to the third floor, he acted surprised to discover she was in 3C, the apartment across the hall from his.

"Well, it sure is a small world," he commented mildly.

"Hmm, yes." She opened her door and paused to glance back at him, uncertainty in her eyes. No doubt good manners had been instilled in her from birth or else she'd have entered and shut the door in his face.

He smiled blandly. Waiting. Would she invite him in?

A thread of hope and dread wound through him. On the one hand, the invitation was exactly what he needed to happen if his plan to become a part of her world was to succeed. But on the other hand, he didn't want to hide who he was from this woman, which was ridiculous. Deception was part of his job. The truth was a moving target. At times it seemed out of reach. He was undercover. Hard stop.

She set her bag down inside the doorway and held out her arms for the bag he carried. Well played. Approving of her continued wariness, he did as she asked, depositing the bag into her waiting hands. She set the bag next to the other inside her apartment entryway.

A white-and-black ball of fluffy cat darted past the bags and Abigail. Before the cat could escape down the hall, Jace scooped up the animal. "Hey, now. Your mama doesn't need any more grief."

He stroked the thick fur until the cat purred and nuzzled into his chest.

"I've never seen her take to a stranger so quick," Abigail said, clearly bemused at her cat's display of attention. "She's usually very aloof until she grows comfortable with a person."

Jace suspected the same was true for the woman. "I have a way with animals. Dogs, cats, horses. I love them all."

She studied him for a moment and then let out a delicate breath. "I don't even know your name."

"Wyatt Prescott, from Austin, Texas, at your service." The words rolled off his tongue with ease, as they had a thousand times before whenever he had to use the alias. Having an undercover ID was a safety precaution and kept his status as a US marshal from the general public. Someone who wanted to get to a witness could use a marshal's family as a way to control the marshal.

"I'm Abby Frost," she said.

"Hello, Abby." He put the cat into her

arms. "You're shaking." His teeth clenched. She wouldn't have suffered such a scare if he'd been on his game. He silently promised it wouldn't happen again. "Maybe you should call someone to come be with you."

Petting the cat, she shook her head. "I've been leaning on my family and friends too much lately."

He snorted. "I'm sure they won't mind."

"No, they wouldn't, but it's the middle of a workday."

Seizing an opportunity, he said, "I can stay with you until someone else can come over." He really needed to know more about her connection to Carlos Reyes and the Ramirez-Estevan family. And he needed to obtain the information covertly.

She stared at him, clearly weighing if she should trust him. Considering she'd just been assaulted, it made sense, but he needed her to trust him. "I promise I'll be a perfect gentleman."

Perfect pearly white teeth worried her bottom lip. "Why should I believe you?"

He figured her distrust went deeper than what had happened this afternoon. "It's good to be cautious. Maybe over time you'll get to know me and conclude I'm a good guy."

She didn't appear convinced. "Maybe."

It was time to retreat. He stepped toward the door across the hall. "I'm right here if you need anything."

Her gaze went to the door and then back to him with a nod. "Thanks. And thank you for today."

He touched the brim of his hat. "My pleasure."

With a hint of a smile, she shut the door.

Great. Now how was he going to gain the information he needed to protect her without giving away the reason he was here?

His phone buzzed in his pocket. His dad. No doubt wanting an update. He'd return the call later. But it did give him an idea.

With his phone in hand, he stepped back to Abby's door and knocked.

She cracked open the door and peeked out at him. "Yes?"

Hoping to appear unthreatening, he said, "I should give you my phone number. Just in case you need—" He refrained from saying *rescuing again*. "Anything."

Her pretty eyes widened. "Oh. Okay. Good idea." She cocked her head and studied him. After a moment of indecision, determination marched across her face. She stepped back, opening the door wider. "Would you like to come in? The least I can do is make you dinner for saving my life."

He had half a mind to tell her she shouldn't invite strangers into her home without properly vetting them, but he nodded and tipped his hat. "Much appreciated."

His plan was coming together perfectly. He stepped over the threshold of her apartment and entered her life. "Thank you for the invitation."

She hurried ahead of him, shrugging out

of her coat. She hung it on a hook beside a set of sliding double doors concealing the washer and dryer.

He closed and locked the door behind him. As he entered the kitchen, similar in layout to his rented apartment across the hall, she quickly picked a few dirty dishes off the counter and placed them in the sink before unloading her grocery bags.

Moving farther into the apartment, he took off the waterproof coat he'd bought at the airport and folded it over the back of a dining room chair. He removed his hat, set it on the seat of the same chair, ran his hand through his hair to get rid of the hat hair and assessed his surroundings.

The apartment was homey in a girlie way, with lots of floral and bright, cheery colors. A plush silver couch sported red-and-white pillows with the motif of various iconic landmarks, such as the Eiffel Tower, Big Ben and the Leaning Tower of Pisa. The walls were adorned with similar prints of various attractions from around the world. Had she visited the many sites? Or was her travel done through images and books?

On the far wall, a bookshelf held an eclectic mix of leather-bound titles and mass-market paperbacks, along with an array of travel books. In the corner, a flat-screen TV sat on a stand. More books had been piled high on the side. The woman was a reader. A trait they shared.

Next to the bookshelf was a collection of framed certificates and plaques. He noted the accolades were academic in nature rather than athletic. She didn't strike him as the competitive type, but she was clearly high achieving.

He made his way back to the kitchen. She lifted a pot from a cupboard, her hands trembling so badly she nearly dropped it.

"Here," he said, rushing to her side. "Let me." He took the pot from her hands.

"I don't know what's wrong with me," she said. "I'm still shaking like a leaf."

"It's the adrenaline dump." He set the

pot aside and took her hands in his. They were ice-cold. He rubbed her slender fingers. "You've had a shock. It's understandable you're upset."

"I suppose you're right." A visible shiver ran over her. "Why did that man attack me twice?"

"What?" Jace's heart jolted. "Twice?"

"This past Tuesday night, the same man tried to grab me outside my work," she said.

"Did you tell the police this?" He couldn't keep the surprised outrage from his tone.

Her gaze narrowed. "Of course. The officer I talked to said today's attack might have been payback for the other night. I used my pepper gel to get away then, but he was prepared for me to use it this time."

A stillness came over Jace. "You said Tuesday night?"

She nodded.

His stomach dropped. She'd called his father on Wednesday morning. Obviously, the cartel had already identified her before her call to the US Marshals Service. Apparently, his father's advice about not contacting the Ramirez-Estevan family had come too late. Jace had studied the Garcia Cartel on the plane ride to the nearby Portland, Oregon, airport. *Vicious* didn't even cover it.

How was Abby, via her biological father, Carlos Reyes, connected to the Ramirez-Estevan family?

If it weren't illegal, he'd hack her computer or the genealogy site. Unfortunately, he didn't have enough for a warrant to compel the company to turn over their records, so Jace needed Abby to trust him. He needed her to allow him to view her DNA profile so he could run background checks on the names she'd connected to. Then he and his father could formulate a plan to ensure Abby Frost, and her family, stayed out of the Garcia Cartel's crosshairs.

Abby couldn't believe how upset Wyatt became after learning this afternoon's attack had been that awful man's second attempt at kidnapping her.

After today, she had no illusions. The man had been intent on taking her away. Abducting her. She'd come close to being a statistic. Another missing woman. Gone without a trace. Her face could have easily ended up on some milk carton or TV crime show.

Her knees wobbled.

"Here, sit." Wyatt led her to the couch.

"But dinner…" she protested without much heat. She doubted she'd be able to eat anyway. Inviting him in and then not being able to prepare him a meal made her inwardly cringe.

The cowboy had saved her life.

For some reason, his calm and charming demeanor put her at ease. An unusual sensation, because she wasn't typically comfortable with strangers. But his presence evoked a sense of safety. And Daisy had accepted him right away. Her cat's endorsement had to count for something, right?

She liked Wyatt's warm, chocolate-colored eyes and strong square jaw. He was tall and thin but definitely muscular beneath the dark blue Henley-style T-shirt. His jeans weren't snug, but they weren't loose, either. Just right. His worn leather cowboy boots left little imprints of the heel in the beige-colored carpet. He'd said he was from Texas, which made perfect sense with his manners and accent. His full head of dark hair would probably curl when he let it grow out. He even sported a big silver belt buckle like she'd seen on the belts of the men on the rodeo channel her best friend, Lisa, sometimes watched.

She'd never met a real-life cowboy before. Oh, there were plenty of men who dressed in jeans, boots and felt hats, but posers, all of them.

The mystique of the honorable, hardworking and charming cowboy had always seemed like a fairy tale to Abby. But she had a hunch this man, Wyatt, was for real.

"Do you know why this man targeted

you?" Wyatt asked as he sat on the edge of the coffee table, facing her with her hands still ensconced within his larger warm ones.

His words jerked her gaze from their joined hands to his eyes. The concern and empathy she encountered surprised her. Why did he care?

Refocusing on his question, she answered, "I don't know. I try to be a good person. Never purposely harm anyone or do anything to cause someone to want to hurt me." She sighed. "I'd never seen that man before he attacked me."

"Is there anything unusual going on in your life?"

Sweat broke out on her brow. "Yes, as a matter of fact. I recently learned my father wasn't my father."

Wyatt's eyebrows rose. "Truly?"

Her shoulders slumped as she revealed her mother's secret. "Mom and this Carlos Reyes guy were in love when they were twenty. They were talking marriage. Then one day, he was gone, and a man from the

US Marshals Service showed up on her doorstep saying Carlos was deceased. No explanation of how or why or where. My mother found out she was pregnant with me a few weeks later."

Squeezing her hands, Wyatt said, "Shocking, I'm sure."

Thankful for his comforting touch, she nodded. "Yes. For my mother then and me now. My parents never told me. They lied to me all these years." She beat back the tears threatening to spill over her lashes. "Learning about Carlos came on the heels of the first attack." Her breath caught. "You don't believe the two are related, do you?"

A shuttered expression entered Wyatt's eyes, darkening them. "I couldn't begin to speculate. But it's definitely something to consider. Can I view the DNA profile?"

She tucked in her chin. "Why?"

His smile oozed so much charm her stomach did a little flip.

"Just curious. I've never done one."

What harm would there be in showing

him? She rose and led him to the dining table, where her laptop sat. She fired up the computer, and they took a seat side by side. He smelled nice, masculine and woodsy. Forcing herself to concentrate and not be distracted by the handsome man sitting so close, she clicked on the email and brought up the report.

"Can you explain the process?"

"Sure. When your DNA analysis is uploaded to the site, you are sent a notice asking if you'd like to see your DNA matches."

"So this is all for public viewing?"

"No, not all. You can make an account public or keep it private. Mine is private, but I can view others who I'm connected to and how much of a DNA match we share. When I accessed mine, then read my sister's DNA profile, I noticed there was a difference."

"How so?"

The truth stung. "We don't share our paternal line."

"Which is how you discovered you have different dads."

She swallowed past the lump rapidly forming in her throat. "Yes."

His blunt fingertip pointed to the screen. "Do you know Paulina Ramirez-Estevan?"

"No. I sent her a note asking to connect but haven't heard back."

"It's certainly intriguing." Wyatt shut the laptop lid. "Why don't I help you make dinner? We could put on some music."

Grateful for the suggestion and the distraction, she smiled. "Let's."

Her sister and her best friend were going to have a field day when they found out Abby had entertained a handsome cowboy, but Abby was a realist. Just because the man had saved her life and she was sharing a meal with him did not mean she could let herself develop any sort of attachments. That way lay peril.

She was a boring banker. Not the adventurous type like her sister, Nancy, or the flirty type like her best friend, Lisa. Most men found Abby too serious. A workaholic. More interested in achieving success than putting energy into a relationship. She was savvy enough to know a man like Wyatt Prescott wouldn't be satisfied with someone like her. She could never be enough.

THREE

Jace stretched and patted his satisfied belly. "Best meal ever."

He sat at Abby's dining room table in her cute little apartment with the cat, Daisy, rubbing against his leg. Jazz music played softly in the background, the sound originating from her laptop and amplified by two wireless speakers. Not his usual genre of music, but he found it oddly pleasing.

Just as he found Abby. He hadn't expected to enjoy spending time with the woman. She had a sharp mind and quick wit. Not to mention she was lovely.

They'd worked side by side to make risotto with spinach and chicken. It was a one-pot dinner and something he'd never considered making. His meals ran more to eggs and bacon or ordering from a local restaurant. The homey scene created a strange ache in his chest. What would it be like to have this kind of domestic and comfortable evening every night? To be with someone so genuine and kind? He'd only just met Abby, but she drew him in and made him ponder about life in a way he had no business doing.

He was a US marshal in the state of Texas on an unsanctioned undercover assignment. When the threat to his protectee was neutralized, his job ended. Then he'd disappear from her life.

But for now, he was here for however long it took to make sure the Garcia Cartel didn't hurt or kidnap her.

If he worked for a different branch of the marshals service or the DEA, ATF or FBI, he'd have a different agenda, one including using this woman as bait to bring down the cartel, but entrapping criminals wasn't his function within the marshals service. His was to protect witnesses and make sure they stayed alive to testify. And then stayed alive after.

This off-the-record assignment had a two-pronged goal—keep Abby alive and keep her from being used by the cartel to draw out Carlos Reyes.

Jace needed to succeed. His father was trusting him, and he wanted to do his father proud.

Abby's cheeks flushed an appealing pink at his praise for her meal. "I'm glad you enjoyed it."

He frowned. "You don't agree?"

"It was just boiled rice with greens and protein." She stood and began to clear the table.

"Not just boiled rice." He rose to help her, taking their glasses to the sink. "There was Parmesan cheese and spices. Mmm. Good stuff."

She slanted him a quick glance, surprise flaring in her eyes. "I can write the recipe down for you."

"Much appreciated." Though preparing

the meal at home in Texas wouldn't be nearly as much fun alone.

"As you witnessed, it's very easy to make."

"Easy, says the woman who knows how to cook." He turned on the water faucet. "I'll wash, you dry?"

"I have a dishwasher." She opened the door to the appliance.

He chuckled. "Then I'll rinse and you load."

She grinned. "Deal."

His gaze snagged on her mouth. She had nice lips. Perfectly formed and unadorned with any color yet arresting just the same. He lifted his gaze to meet hers. He liked the array of green, brown and gold tangled in her eyes. "Do you like country?"

Her brow wrinkled. "What?"

"Country music?"

"Oh, maybe. I'm not sure," she said.

He moved to her laptop, where she had a music app open. With a few clicks, he had a country song filling the apartment.

He sang along as he continued to help with the dishes.

He caught her soft smile and stopped singing. "Sorry."

"No, please, keep singing. I don't mind." She leaned past him to put a dish in the sink.

The floral scent of her shampoo teased his senses, stirring his blood. He really should step back, but he couldn't seem to make his feet move. She glanced at him and stilled, her eyes flaring, her lips parting. She really did have kissable lips.

Whoa. Inappropriate. Not cool.

He was here working, here to protect her, not here to date her. Not to mention she had no idea who he really was. That was the job. Deception was part and parcel of who he was and what he did.

One of his favorite up-tempo songs came on. He grinned and sang with gusto, despite the fact he couldn't carry a tune. She laughed and leaned back against the counter. Her smile created a warm spot in the middle of his chest. Her whole face lit up. Enthralling.

"I know this one," she said and joined in, adding her lilting voice to his.

The song ended, but she still held him enthralled with her gaze. He found himself charmed by her. She was feisty, yet her vulnerability tugged at him. And the way she'd blushed when he'd paid her a compliment earlier touched his heart. It had been so long since he'd enjoyed spending time in the company of a woman who wasn't family or a coworker.

Her lips parted. "Wyatt?"

His alias on her lips slammed reality into focus. She was his to protect. Getting emotionally attached would only backfire on him and could cost her dearly.

Her phone rang.

A good time to exit. "I better go."

"Wait," she said and hurried to her purse. She answered and told the person on the other end of the line she'd call them back. She walked back toward him, so soft and appealing, her honey-blond hair loose about her shoulders, her eyes luminous in the soft glow of the table lamp.

Swallowing back his attraction, Jace retrieved his hat and jammed it on his head. "You didn't have to put your caller off on my account."

"That was Lisa, my best friend," she said. "I can talk to her later."

"I'm glad you have a good support system," he said, meaning it.

"I do—Lisa, my sister and my mom."

He backed toward the door. "Nice." He took the phone from her hand, put in his cell number and handed it back to her. "I've overstayed my welcome. Promise me you'll lock this behind me."

A furrow appeared between her eyes. "Of course."

He retreated before he gave in to the yearning to pull her into his arms and kiss her frown away. He stepped out of her apartment and into the hall. "Good night."

"Good night, Wyatt, and thank you again for saving my life." She shut the door.

The softly spoken words reminded him of his purpose. Protect Abby.

He waited until he heard the soft *snick* of the lock going into place, and then he released the breath crowding his chest. He was digging himself in deep. He really needed to take stock of the situation. Abby Frost was off-limits for so many reasons.

She had no idea who he really was or why he had ingratiated himself into her life. She was in danger and certainly didn't need the added stress of his attraction. There would come a day when he would walk back out of her life as quickly as he'd entered. It was imperative he stay professional.

He'd never been one to abide by all the rules, but succeeding at this assignment was more important than his need to color outside the lines.

And he'd best keep his goal in mind.

He opened the door to his rented apartment. Thankfully, the guy who'd vacated had agreed to leave his furnishings, minimalistic as they were. Jace much preferred the coziness of Abby's place. He hung his hat on a coat hook and belatedly realized he'd left his jacket at Abby's.

Had his subconscious made him forgetful on purpose to give him an excuse to be near her again?

If so, it was only because seeing her repeatedly was part of his job.

He grabbed his phone and called his father.

His dad answered on the first ring. "About time."

Grimacing, Jace said, "Sorry. It's been a hectic day." He told his father about the attack, as well as the previous incident and what Abby had told him about the Ramirez-Estevan connection. He left out his dinner at Abby's and how good a time he'd had in her company. Those were private moments he wasn't willing to share. He refused to examine why.

A grunt of frustration from his father came through the line. "I have to find Carlos. I've put feelers out for word on him through the various law enforcement channels, but he's gone to ground so low his name hasn't popped on any databases."

A potentially fruitless endeavor. "What's being done about the cartel?"

"Believe me, there are more agencies working to bring down Garcia than I can count on two hands," Gavin said. "Convincing Carlos to testify would go a long way. There is no statute of limitations on murder."

"But Carlos's testimony won't keep Abby safe," Jace said, the truth settling like a cold stone around his neck. "Unless they both go into the program."

A conversation he dreaded having with Abby. She had a good life here—friends, family, a job. It was a lot to ask someone to give up. Especially when she had never met the man whose existence now threatened her life.

"Abby will always be leverage to be used against Carlos as long as the man lives," Jace said. "Besides, we don't know if he'll care one way or the other about her.

He might be willing to throw her to the wolves to save his own hide."

A moment of silence stretched. "The only way to keep them both permanently safe is if the Garcia Cartel goes down and their power is stripped away," Gavin said. "Tomas Garcia behind bars would be the best retirement gift of all."

Jace nearly dropped the phone. "You're considering retirement? Since when?"

"It's something your mother and I have been discussing for a while," Gavin said. "We were going to tell you this weekend."

Instead of going home to the family ranch, Jace had been sent to the Pacific Northwest. The home-cooked meal he'd been anticipating had been with Abby instead. A boon he hadn't expected but appreciated.

"We'll talk more about my retirement another time," Gavin stated. "For now, we stick to the plan. You stay vigilant. Keep Miss Frost safe but stay under the radar. We don't want the Garcia Cartel to know we know they are after her."

"It will come out at some point." A thread of unease wove through him. How would Abby respond to learning the source of the threat against her?

"Hopefully, we can make some significant arrests by then," his father said. "I'll reach out to some back channels in the DEA and ATF. There has to be a way to combine forces without tipping off the cartel so we can put an end to their reign of terror. I'll have to be careful. The cartel had someone giving them intel before. There's no way to know if the traitor is gone or if there aren't others now on Garcia's payroll."

Jace sent up a silent prayer for his father's success. Otherwise, Jace was either going to have to stay in Washington permanently, or Abby was going to have to disappear into WITSEC. Neither was a good option.

He hung up with his father and set out to do a perimeter check of the building. He stepped out of his apartment as quietly as he could and eased his way down the three flights of stairs. The main doors in and out of the apartment building were secure.

Though if someone really wanted in, they could finagle an unsuspecting tenant into buzzing them through or break the glass doors. There were security cameras pointed at the entrances, and he was gratified he could count on a video recording of any comings and goings.

In the laundry room in the basement of the building, a cold breeze traipsed across his neck. Muddy footprints smeared the tile floor. He traced the source of cold air to an open ground-level window. A streak of alarm raced along his limbs.

Someone had breached the building.

Abby paced across her living room with the phone to her ear. "I've never had such a good time."

The confession to Lisa sent a confusing mix of delight and apprehension through her. She was afraid to trust something bad wouldn't happen to ruin whatever had started between her and Wyatt. Though, really, she was being beyond silly to envision her rescuer developing tender emotions for her.

Sure, he'd enjoyed her food. And she'd enjoyed cooking with him. He'd been so patient and kind, fun to talk to and good at putting her at ease. The way he'd unabashedly sung off-key had charmed her and prompted her to sing along. There'd been a moment when she'd thought—hoped—he would kiss her. And then he didn't. She stuffed the disappointment aside. Saving her life was enough.

"I can't wait to meet the man who has finally snagged your attention," Lisa said.

"I'm sure you will eventually," Abby assured her and couldn't suppress a smile at Lisa's predictable gasp. Though she hated bursting Lisa's overly romantic bubble by adding, "He lives across the hall."

"Convenient," Lisa said, clearly not thwarted at all. "You'll have to borrow some sugar."

"I have sugar."

Lisa laughed. "As an excuse to see him again."

"Oh." Abby wasn't used to flirting or dating. "Do people really borrow sugar?"

"I don't know, but why not?" Lisa said. "Are you coming to church? You should invite your cowboy."

"He's not *my* cowboy," she said. But the idea of inviting him to the Sunday service did appeal. Was he a man of faith? Something she should find out before she let herself become too comfortable. Faith could make or break a relationship. She'd seen it happen with some of her friends. And she wouldn't settle for less than a man who loved God.

She really did hope Wyatt was a man of faith.

A knock sounded at her door. She stilled. "Someone's at my door."

"Stay on the line with me while you answer," Lisa said, her voice taking on a grave tone.

Abby moved to the door and peered through the peephole. She stepped back, her heart rate ticking up. "It's him," she whispered into the phone.

"Your new neighbor? Nice," Lisa said. "He can't stay away. Hmm. Call me and let me know what happens." She disconnected without waiting for Abby's response.

Another knock rattled her door, more insistent this time.

Holding the phone in one hand, Abby opened the door with the other.

Wyatt stared at her, his eyes dark and his jaw firm. "Are you okay?"

His question and his demeanor sent a tremor through her. "Yes. Is something wrong?"

He let out a noisy breath. "No. Everything's good."

Why didn't she believe him? "Then why are you at my door asking if I'm okay?"

He blinked and stared over her shoulder into the apartment. "My jacket."

Really? He'd seemed upset. Over leaving his coat behind? "Wyatt, please, tell me what's wrong."

He scrubbed a hand over his face. "Honestly, I'm being paranoid. I went to the basement to check out the laundry room and there was a window open. Someone had come in through it."

Something inside of her melted a little even as a shiver of fear prickled her skin. "And you were worried about me? You're so sweet."

Making a face, he said, "*Sweet* is not an adjective I've ever been called."

"Well, now you have." Suddenly, she didn't want to be alone anymore. She stepped back. "Would you like some rocky road ice cream?"

He put a hand over his heart as he stepped into the apartment. "You know my weakness."

Smiling, she closed the door behind him. As he hung his hat on a peg by the door, she went into the kitchen to get out the ice cream and bowls. After scooping out generous portions of the dessert, they settled on her couch, each taking an end cushion, which allowed Daisy to settle in the middle. "I was going to watch a rom-com, but we can find an action-adventure movie."

Digging his spoon into the ice cream, he said, "I'm down for a rom-com."

"You are?"

He grinned. "I'm secure in my manhood."

She jerked her gaze away from his handsome face. He was only a friend. A new male friend. One who seemed to suck up the air in the room and make her breathless with his mere presence. To distract herself, she thumbed the remote and found the movie she had cued up on her streaming device. As the movie started, she settled back, enjoying the companionship and the ice cream.

"Abby?"

Her eyes fluttered. She sat up as Wyatt took her bowl from her and turned off the television, where the credits for the movie had been rolling by. Heat crept up her neck. "Oh, no. I fell asleep, didn't I?"

"You did," he said gently. "It's okay. You had a stressful day." He took their bowls to the kitchen, rinsed them and put them in the dishwasher.

She wanted to crawl into a hole. How could she doze off with Wyatt here? Maybe a testament to how secure and comfortable she'd become with him around.

"I'll say good-night for real, this time," he said, moving toward the door and taking his hat off the peg. "Come lock up behind me."

Forcing her languid legs to move, she approached the door, snagging his jacket from the dining area chair as she did and handing it to him.

He smiled, tipped his hat and left. She shut the door behind him, threw the lock and pressed her forehead to the cool surface.

"Lord, I don't know what to think about all of this," she whispered. "I could really use some clarity."

She pushed away from the door and headed for her bedroom. A few minutes later, a soft knock had her practically skipping back to the door. What excuse would Wyatt use this time?

She opened the door, saying, "Did you forget something el—"

The words died in her throat.

A man she didn't recognize stood there. Tall, menacing, with a beard and dark hair beneath a navy hoodie. He pushed his way in, his hand grabbing for her.

Abby screamed.

The intruder lunged forward and clamped a hand over her mouth. "You scream again, and I'll gut you. Understand?"

A knife in his hand glinted in the hall light spilling into the entryway. Panic seized the breath in her lungs.

She nodded her understanding, her gaze riveted to the sharp blade. Stark fear cramped her insides.

Shutting the door and then locking it behind him, the assailant gripped her biceps and propelled her backward through her entryway into the living room until she was sitting on the couch.

"Tell me where Carlos Reyes is," the man's gruff voice demanded.

She sucked in a shocked breath and shook her head. "He's dead."

The goon narrowed his obsidian eyes. "No," the man snapped. "Where is he?"

"I don't know," she said. "I was told he was dead."

"You better stop lying to me and tell me where to find him, or people will die, starting with your nosy neighbor!"

Abby's heart contracted painfully in her chest. She wished she had answers for this man, but she didn't. And now Wyatt was in danger because of her.

FOUR

Jace heard a female scream abruptly cut off.

Abby.

Gun in hand, he yanked open the apartment door and took a cautious glance into the hallway. Empty.

Heart thumping against his rib cage in a chaotic rhythm, he stilled and listened. He moved to Abby's door and pressed his ear against the wood. From inside, the sound of a male voice, the words muffled by the door and distance, rocked Jace with unadulterated fear and rage. He prepared to kick down the door and then stopped himself. If he went in hot, with gun blazing, Abby could be caught in the cross fire.

Reining in the urge to storm Abby's

apartment, he quickly tucked his weapon into his waistband and returned to his apartment, where he grabbed a small soft-sided, zippered leather case from a pouch in his duffel bag. He hurried back to Abby's door. With nimble fingers, he plucked two slim metal tools from the case, crouched down and went to work on the lock.

Forcing a calmness he hadn't known he possessed, he undid the lock with a soft *snick*. Carefully, he turned the knob and eased the door open until he could slip inside the apartment. Grateful for the shadowed entryway, he closed the door but didn't latch it, afraid the sound would alert the intruder.

"I don't know what you're talking about." Abby's voice wobbled. "Please, you have to believe me."

"How can I?" a rough male voice demanded. "The boss says you're proof he lives."

Still in a crouch, Jace moved farther into the apartment. Daisy sat under the dining room table and meowed softly as if to say, "Hurry up."

"No," Abby said. "He didn't know about me."

"Liar!" The thug's palm connected with Abby's cheek.

The sight of the man hitting Abby filled Jace with fury the likes of which he'd never experienced. It was an unstoppable beast demanding retribution. He vaulted across the room, tackling Abby's assailant. Jace's momentum sent them crashing down onto the coffee table. They rolled onto the floor with a jarring thud. A knife flew from the intruder's hand and disappeared beneath the couch. The wiry man elbowed Jace in the teeth, snapping his head back and sending pain reverberating down his spine.

With a growl, Jace landed a hard punch to the man's gut and then followed with a sharp side-hand chop to the throat, not hard enough to kill, but with enough force to disable. The man reacted as expected, abandoning the fight to claw at his bruised and sore trachea.

Jace took advantage of the moment to withdraw his sidearm and press the barrel to the guy's skull. "Don't move."

Malice radiated from the dark-as-coal eyes staring back at Jace.

Jace searched for Abby and found her already with the phone in her hand. Her wide, shocked eyes were on him as she spoke to the 911 dispatcher.

Keeping a good distance from where Jace had the intruder pinned beneath him on the ground, Abby said, "Wyatt? Who are you?"

Jace gritted his teeth. "Not now."

He couldn't let this thug know his true identity or his true purpose for being in Washington State for fear the goon would report back to the Garcia Cartel. They couldn't know Abby was under the protection of the US Marshals Service. The way Abby's eyes narrowed and her delicate jaw firmed with obvious anger told

Jace in no uncertain terms a moment of reckoning was coming.

Unfortunately, he wouldn't be able to give her the answers she wanted or deserved. Not if he was to stay true to his mission, which was to keep her safe and in the dark.

Heart still racing from the assault, Abby drummed her fingers on the kitchen counter as the Camas police took away the awful intruder who had threatened her life and that of her neighbor, Wyatt. She should be exhausted, but her body was wired with tension. Her mind grappled to understand how this could be happening. Why had she been attacked again? How had the man known about her connection to Carlos Reyes? And why would anyone believe Carlos was still alive?

The assailant had asked for a lawyer when Wyatt demanded to know who'd sent him, and the guy had repeated the request to the Camas officers.

How had Wyatt known her attacker was acting on behalf of someone else?

Who, exactly, was Wyatt?

Certainly not just a cowboy. He'd said he was from Texas. Maybe this was how they did things in the Lone Star State, but it didn't sit well with her.

No, there was something more to Wyatt than met the eye. Even the Camas police sensed it. One of the officers had drawn Wyatt aside, and they'd talked in hushed voices.

The police were gone now, and she was left with Mr. Tall, Handsome and Mysterious. It was time to get to the bottom of things. "Who are you? Really?"

Wyatt ran his fingers through his dark, thick hair. His gaze remained unreadable. "Just a guy from Texas. Nothing special."

She scoffed. Everything about this man was special. "I doubt it very much. You know more than you're letting on."

"I assure you, I'm from Texas," he said, his drawl thickening.

"Okay. I'll believe you're from Texas.

But you're more than just a cowboy from Texas, aren't you?" Not for a second did she believe he was some ordinary guy. "You're law enforcement."

His brow furrowed, his gaze darkening. "What makes you say that?"

"Only every TV show I've ever watched."

He barked out a laugh. "You can't take TV as reality."

"Maybe not. But there is enough realism to know when somebody's been trained to do what you just did." She arched an eyebrow. "Besides, I attended a self-defense class with our local sheriff's department. There's something very similar about you and the deputies who taught our class. The swagger… The confidence…" She was surprised she hadn't realized it sooner. "Whatever it is, you have it."

A grin broke out on his handsome face. "I'm a Texan. We come into the world with swagger and confidence."

His charming smile made her heart thump in an altogether new, strange way, but she refused to let his teasing get to her. "How did you know the intruder was here?"

His grin faded. "I heard you scream."

The scream had come from the darkest, scariest place a woman could experience. She swallowed back the memory of the attack and her foolishness in opening the door without her usual caution of checking the peephole. For the third time in a week, she'd been assaulted. Were the other two incidents related to her biological father, as well? How could they not be? Was he really alive? Who was after him? Why? How had they found her? So many questions rattled around inside her brain. Keeping her focus on Wyatt, she persisted. "Why are you carrying a gun?"

"Again, I'm a Texan."

She rolled her eyes. "After the police pulled you aside, they seemed almost deferential, which only confirms my suspicion you are some sort of lawman."

He held her gaze for a long minute but didn't say anything.

Frustration beat at her temples, and she

considered stepping away to take something for the brewing headache, but she wasn't about to let this conversation go. "You asked that man who'd sent him. How do you know he was working for someone else?"

"You told the officers the suspect was asking about Carlos Reyes."

She shook her head. "You asked him before I spoke to the officers."

A muscle ticked in Wyatt's strong jaw.

She tucked in her chin as an idea formed. "That's why you're here? You also believe my biological father is still alive, and you're hoping I'll lead you to him."

A slight grimace crossed his handsome face. He shifted his weight in an unmistakable attempt to regain his composure. "Obviously, someone believes Carlos Reyes is alive," Wyatt said. "Or that man wouldn't have broken into your apartment demanding to know the location of Reyes's hidey-hole."

Though he didn't outright confirm her suspicion, she was correct. Wyatt was in

Washington searching for Carlos Reyes. A deep sense of betrayal sliced through her. Not nearly as deep as her mother's omission of the circumstances of Abby's birth, but still a wound to her heart. She'd started to let down her guard and had even hoped she could maybe have something romantic with Wyatt. But his coming to her rescue twice now was no coincidence. Who was she kidding? She didn't believe in coincidence. Had God sent this man to protect her?

Or was he someone for her to fear?

No. She dismissed the question almost as quickly as it had surfaced. If Wyatt had wanted to harm her, he could have done so by now, but he'd been a gentleman. While she was grateful to be alive and thankful Wyatt had come to her aid, she wished he'd been honest with her from the beginning. Then she wouldn't have set herself up for heartache. "Again, I'm asking you who—or rather, what—are you?"

"It's better if we don't travel down that particular road."

Not about to let him put her off, she declared, "You are law enforcement."

He arched an eyebrow.

She replayed the events of the past few days and gasped as realization slid into place. "You're with the US Marshals Service."

His eyebrows shot up nearly to his hairline. "What makes you think so?"

It made so much sense. "Because you showed up after I called deputy US marshal Gavin Armstrong." She frowned. "But you can't be Deputy Armstrong. You're too young."

Wyatt pressed his mouth into a straight line.

She narrowed her gaze. "It will be easy enough for me to confirm." She marched across the room to where her phone sat charging and quickly found the number to the US Marshals Service she had dialed a few days ago.

A big, warm hand closed over hers. "Abby."

Facing him, she searched his deep brown eyes. "I deserve to know the truth."

His expression softened, his eyes glowing with tenderness and regret. "Let me make a phone call."

At least she was making progress. "Get on with it, then, Wyatt."

Jace grimaced. It was tough hearing her use his alias. That she'd already guessed he was with the US Marshals Service spoke to the woman's intelligence. He'd already known she was smart, but he'd underestimated her ability to puzzle out the truth. He couldn't deny his relief she was safe. Taking down the intruder had been satisfying, but the thug hadn't given up any useful information. Not that Jace needed confirmation the Garcia Cartel was trying to get information on Carlos. Who else would it be?

"Well, Wyatt? If that is even your real name."

Abby's stare settled in his chest. Guilt, an unusual sensation when he was on a case, bloomed. He did what he had to do to get the job done. He couldn't reveal his identity to her, not yet. Though the desire for her to know the real him was strong.

Trepidation tripped down his spine. He was going to have to confess to his father he'd made a mess of this. But it couldn't be helped. He took his phone from his pocket and stepped into the hallway. He wasn't about to call his father with Abby listening. He dialed his dad's cell phone. On the second ring, Gavin picked up. "Jace."

"Hey." Jace glanced toward Abby, who leaned against the kitchen counter. Anger and expectations snapped in her pretty eyes. So much for some privacy.

Turning his back to her and lowering his voice, he said into the phone, "We have a situation. Abby—uh, Abigail Frost— was attacked in her home. The suspect demanded to know where Carlos Reyes was hiding."

His father growled into the phone. "This complicates things."

"More than you know. Abby has reasoned out my connection to the US Marshals Service."

His father heaved a heavy sigh. "Would she be content to let it go if you tell her we are handling the situation?"

"Doubtful." Even though he'd only known Abby for a short span of time, he had the distinct impression she would not let the truth remain hidden. And, frankly, he didn't blame her. Her life was on the line. The Garcia Cartel was making it clear they wanted answers and were convinced she had them.

"Is that Deputy Armstrong?"

Abby's voice coming from right behind Jace had him stiffening. He turned to find her hovering inches from his right shoulder. He adjusted the phone to his left ear.

"I heard," his father said. "There's no hope for it. You'll need to bring her here. This isn't a conversation we should have over the phone. Especially not on an unsecured line."

Jace's stomach dropped. He wasn't sure Abby would agree to going to Texas, but somehow he had to make her trust him again. "How much can I reveal?"

"The basics. We can get into the details when you get here. There's a transport leaving PDX headed to Austin in two hours. Be on it. I'll have someone meet you."

His dad assumed convincing Abby to up and leave with him via Portland International Airport would be an easy feat. "I'll do my best. What about her mother and sister?"

There was a moment of silence. Then his father said, "I'll send locals to watch over them until we have a better plan." He hung up.

Jace disconnected and met Abby's gaze. She was a force to be reckoned with when upset. He liked that she wasn't in hysterics or even shedding tears. She had a strong backbone. She was going to need it for what was coming.

"How do you feel about going to Texas?"

Her eyebrows shot up. "Excuse me? Why would I need to go to Texas?"

"If you want answers, Texas is where you'll find them."

"You asked how much you can reveal. So start revealing."

He gestured toward the living room. "Take a seat." He needed a moment to collect his composure.

Abby moved to the couch and stopped with her back to him and her head slightly bowed. Was she praying?

A good idea. He lifted a silent prayer of his own, asking God to give him the words. And to allow Abby an open heart to hear them.

He squared his shoulders. Best to just get it done. He joined her in the living room. At his approach, she sat primly on the edge of the couch cushion. He grabbed a dining room chair, scooted it closer and turned the chair around to straddle it, resting his arms over the back. "Here's the deal. Yes, I am with the marshals service. My boss sent me to protect you." All true. Now came the tricky part. "When working undercover, I have an assumed identity."

Her face remained impassive. Her gaze steady on him. He noticed the little pulse point at the base of her throat. She may appear outwardly calm and collected, but her heart was racing. Another niggle of guilt tickled his conscience.

"You're not Wyatt Prescott."

She'd discover the truth of his identity when they reached Texas. Better to tell her now instead of waiting. "No. I'm deputy US marshal Jace Armstrong."

"Jace Armstrong."

His name on her lips did funny things to his insides. He hoped revealing his identity would go a long way to regaining her trust. The intensity of the need for her to trust him caught him by surprise. "Yes."

"Deputy Gavin Armstrong is your father?"

He dipped his head. "And my boss. Though he is now Marshal Armstrong."

A moment of perplexity crossed her

pretty face. Clearly, she didn't understand the significance.

"He was promoted."

"Ah. Okay." Still appearing confused, she said, "Is Carlos Reyes alive? Why can't you just explain to me what's going on?"

The frustration and anxiety in her voice battered at him. He wanted to appease her, to lay out the situation and make her aware of the stakes involved. And if this weren't his father's old case, Jace would tell Abby all of it, but the story wasn't his to tell. "This is a highly classified and sensitive case. If you want to know more, you'll come with me. The choice is yours."

For a long moment, she sat still and silent. Her gaze never wavered. "What if the people who came after me go after my mom or my sister? What do I tell them?"

"My boss is making arrangements for their protection."

A little V appeared between her eyebrows. "I need to warn them."

"It would be a mistake at this juncture.

Once we reach the San Antonio office and you understand the ramifications, then you can choose what you'd like to do and how much you want to reveal."

She shook her head. "No. I'm not going to disappear without telling them what is going on. What would you do if you were in my shoes?"

The words hit him square in the gut. He couldn't fault her for wanting to protect her family. He'd do the same. If the cartel did make a move on Abby's mom and sister, the worst-case scenario would be the three women could all go into witness protection. "Make the call, but don't mention Carlos Reyes. We don't know if he is alive, and you don't want to upset your mother needlessly."

Abby gave a humorless laugh. "Right. How else can I explain what's happening? My mother is strong. She'll be okay."

He hoped for her sake she was correct. "Can you make arrangements to take a few more days off from work? Tell your boss you're taking a vacation and arrange for someone to take your cat. We'll leave for Texas on the next transport in a few hours."

She took her phone and disappeared into the bedroom. After a moment, the cadence of her soft voice seeped under the door frame.

He paced the length of her living room, unwilling to leave her long enough so he could pack. She was going to have to accompany him across the hall. He'd almost lost her twice now. He wouldn't be so careless again.

Twenty minutes later, she returned from her bedroom carrying an overnight bag. "My friend Lisa will come over and get Daisy. I called my boss at home. He's fine with me taking some of my vacation days, though he wasn't thrilled at being awoken so early. My mom and sister are naturally upset but will cooperate."

"What did you tell them?"

She gave him a defiant stare. "The truth. Or as much of it as I know."

A smiled tugged at his mouth. Her integrity was admirable. Respect blossomed within his chest. "All righty then. If you'll come with me to the apartment across the hall, I'll pack my things."

She preceded him out of her apartment and locked the door behind them.

Remaining in the entryway while he quickly repacked his duffel bag, she asked, "How did you get Mack to leave?"

"I told you the truth. He received a transfer and a nice bonus for cooperating."

Thankfully, Jace hadn't made himself too comfortable yet. They were on their way to the Portland airport within minutes. There was little traffic leaving the town of Camas so early in the morning. The predawn sky was clear and filled with stars, but the silence invading the cab of the rental truck was thick as fog. Gone was the easy camaraderie they'd shared earlier in the evening. Unaccountably, he missed it. Strange. He usually did a much better job of compartmentalizing his job and his private life.

Something about Abby got under his

skin. He couldn't say it was her vulner-ability, though she did have a vulnerable side. Her strength of character touched him and made him more determined to protect her. He sent up a silent prayer, ask-ing God to soothe her hurt feelings so they could get back on better footing, because it would make the process easier for them both.

He glanced in the rearview mirror, con-vinced the twin headlights behind him had been there from the moment they pulled out of her apartment building parking lot. He took the on-ramp for the freeway, quickly speeding up. The vehicle behind them did the same. As they drove onto the bridge crossing the Columbia River, the vehicle behind them accelerated until it was nearly kissing their bumper.

Jace had the gas pedal floored and was thankful the traffic was light going into Oregon as he sliced across the four lanes with the other car keeping pace. They were almost to the exit for the airport when the sedan behind them changed lanes abruptly and rammed into the back end of the truck, trying to make the bigger vehicle spin out of control.

With grim determination, Jace spun the wheel into the turn, pointing the truck in the direction of the slide to maintain traction as they spun. Beside him, Abby let out a strangled sound as she clung to the door handle. Keeping control of the vehicle and once again facing the correct direction, he stomped on the brakes, letting the offending car swoosh past them.

Jace caught a glimpse of a weapon sticking out through the open window as the vehicle went by. Fearing for Abby, he stepped on the gas and jerked the steering wheel just as shots rang out.

FIVE

The echo of gunfire shuddered through Abby, and she clung to the truck's door handle with all her might as Jace veered across the freeway lanes, then took the airport exit off-ramp, the headlights illuminating the dark road. Horns blared, and tires screeched on the wet pavement around them. She held her breath, expecting flying glass or a bullet to rip through her, but neither happened.

Jace merged onto another off-ramp. The frontage road paralleled a private airstrip where charter airplanes were housed. She frowned at him. "We're taking a private plane?"

"Correct. A JPATS plane."

He didn't slow the truck or pull into the

parking lot of the charter plane terminal. Instead, he continued until they were at a metal fence with a large rolling gate. Jace pulled up to a manned gatehouse, stopped and rolled down his window. He showed his credentials to the uniformed guard. Using a flashlight, the guard studied them both.

"I'm transporting a witness," Jace said.

The guard ducked back inside the gatehouse, consulted a computer and then waved them through.

Abby twisted in her seat, tracking the gate as it closed behind them. "And just what kind of plane is a JPATS?"

Without shifting his attention from the road, he said, "Justice Prisoner and Alien Transportation System."

She swallowed hard. "So, not a vacation travel company?"

He grunted and deftly drove the silver truck across the tarmac toward a waiting plane. Bright lights shone on a medium-sized all-white jet with numbers on the back end and a US flag on the tail. There were five men wearing orange jumpsuits huddled together on the tarmac near the base of rolling metal stairs surrounded by men and women wearing dark rain slickers with the words *US MARSHAL* on the back.

Her gaze shot to Jace as he brought the truck to a halt. "No way. I'm not getting on a plane with men in shackles."

He slanted her a glance from beneath the brim of his cowboy hat. "It's safer than flying commercial."

Surely he'd meant to say *scarier*. "Safer for whom?"

He twisted in his seat to face her and took her hands in his. Warmth ran up her arms. The rough calluses on his palms confirmed her suspicion being a cowboy wasn't just an affectation for this man.

"Abby, you're going to have to trust me on this."

Yet he'd lied to her. She didn't like deception or the pain it caused.

"Stay put. I'll be right back." He opened

the door and hopped out before she could form a protest.

Through the smattering of rain hitting the front windshield, she tracked him as he jogged over to two of the marshals. While they conferred, she worried the strap of her purse. What offenses had the shackled men committed? Where were they going? Would the plane crash? Would the convicts riot?

So many awful scenarios played in her head, making her shiver with fright.

"Stop it!" she told herself. She breathed in, trying to calm the chaotic maelstrom taking hold of her mind.

Don't awfulize, she scolded herself. *Be strong*. She didn't consider herself strong. She was in over her head. What was she doing? Flying thousands of miles for details regarding a man she didn't know and who'd put her in jeopardy. It was an outlandish plan, yet something inside drove her to find answers.

If she had time to process, she'd probably back out. Still could. However, by the time Jace returned to the truck, she was antsy to get going. She needed the truth of who she really was, and the truth was in Texas.

When Jace returned, he retrieved his duffel bag from behind the driver's seat, pulled out a dark blue jacket similar to the ones being worn by the other US marshals and laid it on her lap. "Put this on."

He also retrieved a baseball cap with the US Marshals emblem on the front panel. "Hide as much of your hair as possible." Then he added a pair of dark sunglasses.

She stared at the items he intended for her to wear. "You really expect this disguise to work? Nobody's going to believe I'm a US marshal."

He flashed her a grin. "It's better for everyone if you're not recognizable."

A shiver of unease slithered over her. Hesitation beat a drum march beneath her breastbone. She swallowed the burst of anxiety clawing up her throat. "I wish you would tell me what's going on. Who are the men after Carlos Reyes? Why do they want me?"

"All in good time." He slung his duffel bag over his shoulder. "Hurry up. We have to get on this plane. They're about to take off."

From her vantage point in the front passenger seat of the truck, she scrutinized the shackled men being escorted onto the plane via the stairs. Did she dare join them? It was decision time.

If she wanted answers, then yes, she had to.

With a deep sigh of resignation and acceptance to cover her anxious flutters, she slipped the jacket on over her sweater and zipped it up to her chin. She dug out an elastic band from her purse, smoothed back her hair into a low ponytail and then tucked the ends under the collar of the jacket. She put on the hat, pushing back stray hairs and tucking them under the edge. She put the glasses on, muting the bright lights of the runway.

Jace opened the passenger door and offered her his hand. Always the gentleman. She didn't want to like him. In fact, she was quite mad at him right now. But her burning need to know why her life was being upended overrode her distrust and her upset. Ignoring his hand, she stepped out of the truck into the misting rain.

He grabbed her bag and then shut the door. "Let's go."

At the stairs leading up to the plane, he paused. "Keep your head down and don't speak."

She made a face at his back but ducked her head as requested.

He preceded her up the staircase. Once on board, the raucous laughter of the prisoners quieted. It was all she could do not to glance up to determine what had caused the stall in noise. However, if the itchy sensation was any indication, they were all staring at her. Jace motioned for her to take the front window seat. She slid into it, grateful to be hidden by the tall backrest. He tucked their bags overhead and then sat down next to her. The noise from the back of the plane resumed.

"How long is—"

Jace held up a hand. "No talking."

She let out a huff of frustration. Soon, the pilot boarded and entered the cockpit. A few moments later, the engines fired to life, filling her ears with their roar. A nervous flurry took residence in her stomach. She was really doing this. Flying across the country to find answers about the man whose blood ran through her veins. She sent up a litany of prayers for her mother and sister's safety.

Once she had the answers to the burning questions inside her, she would be able to let this go and move on with her life.

Beside her, Jace settled back, dipping his cowboy hat low over his forehead and closing his eyes.

Really? He was going to sleep?

She placed her elbow on the armrest and her chin in her hand and stared out the window. As the plane took off, climbing higher and higher in the sky, she questioned if she'd made the right decision.

Was knowing the truth about her father worth the risk of leaving her world behind?

Jace awoke to a poke in the ribs. Morning sunlight filled the plane cabin, stinging his eyes. He turned his head to stare at Abby. The sunglasses hid her eyes, but the sweet curve of her lips had his heart pumping. The plane engine wound down, and the drop of elevation pitched his stomach as they headed toward the Austin airport runway reserved for the JPATS jet.

Clearing his throat, he sat up, groggy but thankful for the few hours of rest. It was a relief to arrive without incident in Texas. Now all they had to do was make it safely to San Antonio, where she could meet with his father, get the answers she sought and then... He didn't know what would happen after. He wished he could predict the future, but he understood only

God was in control. Jace had to trust there was a plan in place.

He tried to make sense of why the cartel had sent men to shoot them. Apparently, they were not opposed to hurting Abby if they couldn't get the answers they wanted from her. Or could this mean they'd found Carlos? Or were they giving up? If they truly believed Carlos was really dead, then why continue to come after Abby? Revenge for being hard to abduct? Revenge against Carlos in absentia?

The seemingly endless loop of questions was interrupted when the jet touched down and taxied to an outbuilding on the outskirts of the airport where the JPATS terminal was located under heavy security. A prison transport bus was the only vehicle on the tarmac. Jace frowned. Where were the marshals who were supposed to take them to San Antonio?

As soon as the engines powered off, one of the marshals transporting the prisoners opened the cabin door. A rolling staircase was pushed up to the plane, making it possible to exit the jet. The marshal gave Jace a nod, indicating for him and his witness to deplane first. Jace stood and grabbed their bags from the overhead compartment and then hustled Abby through the door and down the stairs.

The early Texas morning heat bounced off the blacktop tarmac and hit him in the face. Sweat broke out on his brow. Amazing what a couple of days away from his home state could do. He'd kind of acclimated to the misty rain and the sweet piney scent of the Pacific Northwest. He inhaled deeply, taking in the familiar bitter aroma of sagebrush and Texas earth.

"Now what?" Abby asked. "Can I take this jacket off? Is it always this hot in October?"

"Pretty much." Propelling her farther away from the plane toward the gate leading to the road, he said, "Don't take the jacket off yet."

He opened his phone to check his messages. His father had sent a text. Two marshals from the Austin office would escort them to San Antonio.

They were late.

The prisoners were put onto the prison transport bus. As it rattled past them, Jace tucked Abby against him, away from the prying eyes of the prisoners.

The two marshals who had been on the plane approached. "Is there a problem?" one of them asked.

"Our transport's behind schedule," Jace told the marshal.

"We can't leave until they get here." The man's voice held a note of censure.

Jace understood. Security at the airport was tight. Despite his credentials, Jace was aware they would be considered a threat until they were escorted off the tarmac.

The rumble of a metal gate opening claimed their attention. A black SUV roared forward, stopping a few feet from where they stood. The passenger door opened, and a man dressed in casual pants with a long-sleeve button-up shirt stepped out. He wore the familiar lanyard with a badge hanging around his neck and a baseball cap on his head matching the one Abby wore. The marshal waved them forward.

Jace nodded his thanks to the two prison transport marshals and hustled Abby to the SUV. Electing to keep their bags with them, Jace helped Abby into the back passenger seat and stuffed her bag on the floorboard at her feet. He climbed in, setting his bag between them, and shut the door.

He caught a glimpse of the driver in the rearview mirror. The man had a wicked-looking scar across his temple. Jace couldn't place the face. And Jace didn't recognize the passenger, either. Unease slithered across his nape. He leaned forward. "Are you two new with the Austin office?"

The men exchanged a glance as the driver shifted the vehicle into Drive and went out the gate.

The passenger replied, "You could say

that. We transferred in from South Carolina."

Jace sat back. Was he being paranoid? Transfers happened all the time. His best friend, Brian, had transferred to the Los Angeles marshals office last year. "What are your names?"

The passenger answered again. "I'm Brady Smith. This is George Jones."

Noticing they weren't taking the more direct route, Jace asked, "Is there something wrong with Interstate 35?"

"There was a horrible accident," Brady said. "It made us late."

Though Jace wanted to accept the explanation, his mind reasoned an accident on the freeway headed toward the airport didn't mean the freeway out of the airport would be congested. He didn't like this one bit. Even if they were headed in the right direction. He slipped his phone from his pocket and sent an SOS text to his father.

The vehicle slowed in the town of Mustang Ridge, and when they bypassed the signs for I-35 west, which would take them directly to San Antonio, every alarm system in his body went off. He had to handle the situation carefully. Abby's life was at stake. He leaned forward again. "Hey, could you stop at a diner? We need to use the facilities."

"You can use them when we arrive," the driver barked out.

His partner, Brady, shot him a vicious glare and then smiled at Jace over his shoulder. "Of course we can stop. We wouldn't want things to get messy in here."

Though the words were innocuous enough and addressed one issue, they were laced with a subtle warning. Abby's hand clamped on his arm in a tight grip. Apparently, she'd discerned the threat, as well.

A fast-food joint loomed up ahead. Jace pointed. "Stop there."

For a moment, Jace didn't believe the driver would comply, but then he slowed, put on the blinker and made the turn into the parking lot. Jace breathed a bit easier.

As soon as the car came to a halt around the back of the building near the bathrooms, Jace popped open his door. He tucked his duffel bag on the floorboard and reached back in the SUV to take Abby's hand. The driver hopped out, opened her side door and made a grab for her.

Jace tugged her toward him. "This way."

Without second-guessing him, she slid across the bench seat, lifting her feet up over his duffel bag and sliding into his arms. He pulled her close and whispered into her ear, "Go use the restroom." He dropped his phone into the pocket of her jacket. "Call my dad. Don't come out until I knock on the door."

She nodded, and he shifted to tuck her into his side as they walked away from the SUV. Their escorts followed. At the women's bathroom, he held open the door for her and then pulled it shut behind her.

Jace needed to get the two men separated. He addressed Brady, who seemed to be the one calling the shots. "We haven't eaten since last night. Could we get a couple of hamburgers?"

The driver, George, growled. Jace shot him a questioning glance. Hopefully, his face didn't reveal his suspicion these two men worked for the Garcia Cartel.

"George, why don't you get us all some grub?" Brady said.

George shot his partner a murderous glare before he stomped away to the entrance of the restaurant.

Jace knocked on the bathroom door. "Abby?"

The door immediately opened. He took her hand and pulled her close. "Let's wait by the vehicle. We're exposed out here."

Brady's gaze narrowed. "You don't need to…?"

"I can wait." He hustled Abby back to the SUV and urged her into the back passenger seat, but he didn't join her.

Brady opened the front passenger door and turned to face Jace.

Knowing he had one shot at this, Jace swiveled to face Brady. In the same motion, he kicked Brady in the gut, throwing him back against the open passenger door. Jace lunged forward and followed up with a one-two punch to Brady's jaw, dropping the man to the ground.

Wasting no time, Jace jumped into the passenger's seat, slammed the door shut and quickly engaged the locks. He climbed across the console into the driver's seat and growled with frustration when he realized George had taken the keys. He quickly hit the button for the satellite road service installed in all of the marshals' vehicles. He identified himself and asked the service to start the car remotely. The engine roared to life. He put the gear into Drive and stepped on the gas just as George ran out the door of the fast-food joint, his gun drawn.

"Down!" Jace shouted to Abby.

The back window exploded. Jace glanced in the rearview mirror. George chased after them, firing bullets into the back of the vehicle. Jace swerved around two cars and drove through the intersection against the red light. Cars honked and tires screeched. He kept going, racing down the highway until the signs for Interstate 35 appeared.

"Can I sit up now?" Abby's muffled voice sounded from the back.

"Yes. Are you okay?"

"I have glass in my hair." In the rearview mirror, he noticed the marshals hat had been knocked from her head. The wind swirling through the interior of the SUV from the broken rear window captured the stray strands of her ponytail, blowing them across her face. Her eyes were big and luminous. He found no hint of hysteria, despite the fear that had leached the color from her face.

"We have to ditch this vehicle," he told her.

He took the next off-ramp, dropping them into the town of San Marcos. Slowing, he searched for a place to stash the SUV. He turned into a strip-mall parking lot, drove around to the back and hid the SUV behind several dumpsters. He helped Abby from the vehicle, grabbed their bags and held out his hand for his phone. She handed it over as they hurried away from the SUV.

"Did you get ahold of my dad?"

"It went to voice mail. I told him we were in trouble and were at a burger place, but I didn't know the name of the town."

Jace dialed his father's number. It had barely rung when his father answered, his voice brimming with concern. "Miss Frost?"

"It's me," Jace said into the phone. "We're in San Marcos. We have to get out of here now."

"I can send people to you."

"No. You once believed there was a mole in the Justice Department. You're right. Two men showed up claiming to be the marshals sent to pick us up at the JPATS terminal, but they were cartel." He gave his dad descriptions of both men and the hardware they carried.

"We might have two dead marshals we may never find." The hard edge to his father's voice matched the anger rioting within Jace.

"These two men showing up confirm your mole is still active and probably monitoring this call," Jace said. "I'm going to ditch this phone. I'll contact you when we get to San Antonio." He hung up, took the SIM card out and broke it in half.

"Now what?" Abby asked.

"We find us some wheels to get us out of here."

"Do you mean we steal a car?"

Jace gave her a half smile. "I'd prefer not to. But extreme circumstances require extreme measures." He glanced around until he spied the perfect vehicle. "This way."

As they neared his choice parked under a tree, Abby's steps faltered. "You've got to be joking."

"It's perfect." The bright orange muscle car had fat tires and big exhaust pipes. "Fast and fun to drive."

"And will draw attention." She glanced around and pointed to a dark blue minivan. "Nothing more inconspicuous than a mom car."

He tilted his head and stared at her. "Have you led a life of crime I don't know about?"

"No, but I watch a lot of police dramas. Inconspicuous would be the way to go."

He barked out a laugh. "As much as I hate to go against what you've learned on television, this car is older, therefore easier to hot-wire. Most modern cars have safeguards against theft."

Her mouth pressed into a thin line. "Fine. Just remember I warned you."

He prayed her warning proved unnecessary.

SIX

As she followed Jace across the parking lot, the knot in Abby's gut tightened, twisting her insides up and making her want to retch. How had everything gone so wrong? Being on a plane with convicts, scenarios of hijackings and crashes playing through her head during the whole flight, had been bad enough, but then they'd been abducted by fake marshals. And now they were going to steal a car. Why stealing a car was the worst of it, she couldn't say.

She just wanted to go home. She should never have started this mess. If only she could rewind time. Go back to when Nancy first suggested they do a DNA test and trace their roots. She'd imagined finding out they had a doctor or a woman suffragist in their ancestry. Discovering she wasn't the true daughter of the man she'd called father her whole life had been completely unexpected.

Jace reached for the door handle of the bright orange souped-up car, and it beeped, the taillights flashing. Abby's heart jolted into overdrive.

A man shouted as he hurried toward them. "Hey, what are you doing?"

"Sorry, man. We were just admiring." Jace snagged her elbow and moved them quickly away from the fancy car.

Abby's blood pumped through her system with aching speed, and she feared she might pop a vein. "Talk about a bad idea."

"You don't need to gloat."

She cringed. "Sorry. Not my intent."

Jace tugged her toward a deli in the strip mall. When they entered the cool shop, her stomach grumbled loudly in response to the smells of spicy mustard and cured meats.

"Let's grab something to eat. My mind

doesn't work so well on an empty stomach." He urged her to a back table in the corner and tucked their bags underneath. "What kind of sandwich would you like?"

Still grappling with the rush of fear and adrenaline comingling with relief, she doubted she'd be able to eat. Yet her mouth watered in response to the delicious smells permeating the air. "Pastrami on rye. Spicy brown mustard. Sauerkraut on the side."

Jace grinned. "A woman after my own heart." He sauntered away to place their orders.

His words shouldn't settle so pleasingly deep inside her. Winning his heart wasn't on her agenda, and she had no business sprouting mushy emotions for the handsome lawman, even if her heart beat just a bit too fast whenever he was close.

He came back and sat down while the sandwiches were being made. Despite her upset at so many things regarding Jace, she couldn't deny she was curious about him and what made him tick. "Why are you a marshal?"

His eyebrows rose. "That's a leading question."

"It's a pretty straightforward question."

Jace seemed to consider her words. "As you know, my father is a marshal. I wanted to follow in his footsteps."

She tapped a finger on the table to contain her annoyance. He probably used the pat answer all the time, but she sensed there must be something more to his choice of career. Men didn't just follow their fathers into whatever line of work without more than parental love guiding them. "No, really. You could have gone into any other aspect of law enforcement. Why follow your father into the marshals service?"

"Are you trying to analyze me?"

"Maybe. It would help me to understand why I should trust you if I know a little bit more about you."

His lips pressed together, and he gave a sharp nod. "I did consider becoming a Texas Ranger. But I believe in what the marshals do. I specifically went into WIT-

SEC because I believe people deserve a second chance."

An admirable sentiment. She couldn't stop the little bump of affection crowding her chest. "Your family must be very proud of you."

"I'd like to hope so." His lips twisted. "But I don't always adhere to the rules."

A small laugh escaped. "Somehow I believe you."

He shrugged. "If the rules don't make sense..."

"You were probably a handful of trouble for your parents."

His grin tugged at her heart. "True that." He gave another shrug. "Sometimes you have to forge through a situation, doing what you need to, for the best possible outcome."

"Does your father operate the same?"

"No, my dad is by the book. I'm the bane of his existence."

"I doubt it." Jace was a straight arrow. Well, except for wanting to steal a car. What other sort of mischief did he regularly get into? "He wouldn't have sent you to protect me if he didn't believe in you. He could've sent someone else. Which does beg the question—why didn't he send a marshal from the Portland or Seattle office?"

"I see what you're doing." He wagged a finger. "We're not talking about your case right now. It's not my story to tell."

Inwardly, she growled. He hadn't taken her bait. Fine. There was more to learn. "Is there a Mrs. Armstrong?"

"There is." His whole face lit up.

A spurt of jealousy erupted and she clenched her jaw.

"My mother is the best."

Heat flooded her face and she pressed, "Do *you* have a Mrs.?"

He placed his hands on the table and tilted his chair onto the back legs. "Are you asking me if I'm married?"

She was. Though she shouldn't be. It didn't matter one way or another to her. She redirected the conversation. "Your mother. What does she make of all this?"

Jace gave her a knowing smile. How could he read her so well?

"Mrs. Armstrong, my mother, is very proud of her husband and son. Though she worries." His gaze darkened. He let the chair drop forward with a clatter on the tile floor, rose and headed to the front of the deli just as the man behind the counter put their order up.

When Jace returned, he set a basket with a delicious pastrami sandwich and a small ramekin of sauerkraut in front of her and one with the same for himself at his spot.

For the next few minutes, they ate in silence. She hadn't realized how famished she was. Apparently, fearing for your life worked up an appetite.

After taking a drink from the water bottle Jace had given her, she stated, "I can understand your mom's worry. What you do is risky. I can attest to the danger."

Jace picked up their empty baskets and carried them away without responding. He was stalling. Abby wasn't going to let him prevaricate. He'd learn once she was on a topic, she wouldn't let go until she was satisfied.

When he returned from throwing their trash away, he didn't sit. "We should move."

Figuring there would be time later for more questions, she complied and grabbed her bag. Once they were out on the sidewalk, she said, "Are you going to try to steal a different car now?"

"No. We're going to catch the Greyhound bus to San Antonio."

She stopped walking. "Won't we be putting other people in danger?"

He urged her on. "Only if our pursuers know we're getting on the bus, but there's no way for them to know. Neither of us has a cell phone. And as you suggested, they may be monitoring police calls. If we steal a car and it's reported stolen, the bad guys would have a bead on us."

His logic made sense. She forced herself to trust his judgment. What choice did she have? They walked at a steady clip for several blocks, taking a few side streets before they found the Greyhound bus stop in front of a clapboard kiosk. Jace went inside and bought two tickets.

"The bus should be arriving within the next twenty minutes," he said when he rejoined her. "Let's go wait in the shade over there." They moved beneath a big magnolia tree, its blossoms sweet and the grass beneath their feet freshly cut.

"So is there a Mrs. Jace Armstrong?"

He slanted her a glance and leaned back against the tree trunk. "No, ma'am."

The news shouldn't fill her with relief, but for some unaccountable reason, it did. "Why not?"

"Why do you want to know?"

Errr. She didn't like when people answered a question with a question. Especially when she didn't want to answer the question. "Just curious about you. Are you one of those love-them-then-leave types? Do you have a string of broken hearts littering a path behind you?" The moment the words left her mouth, her heart began to thump hard in her chest. She had no business probing his personal life. He was here to do a job. End of story.

"Hardly." He gave a self-effacing laugh. "If you must know, I did have a serious girlfriend. But she found somebody who could give her the life she wanted, which wasn't being hitched to a lawman."

Warm pleasure spread through Abby's chest, and she quickly tamped it down. "I'm sorry."

He shrugged. "Don't be. I'll admit my ego was bruised, but the whole experience made me realize marriage, and all that goes with it, is not for me. It's too much hassle and heartache. I don't want a woman to go through the agony and loneliness my mother endures."

She frowned, not liking the disappointment seeping through her. His decision shouldn't affect her. He wasn't her concern. But still, the fact he regarded romance and love so harshly didn't sit well. Surely his mother didn't regret marrying Jace's father and having Jace?

"What about you?"

Jace's voice wrapped around her, making her gaze snap back to his.

"What about me?"

"Why isn't there a Mr. in your life?"

Her mouth dried. He'd neatly turned the tables on her. She deserved it, she supposed. "What does it matter?"

His grin was lopsided and full of mischief. "It might help me know how best to protect you if I know you a bit better."

He was using her logic on herself. She didn't like it, but she figured it was probably fair. Except she didn't know how to respond. She could give him a pat answer—like she hadn't found Mr. Right yet. But the truth was she'd taken herself off the market and had no plans to put herself out there anytime soon. It had hurt too much when she'd realized she would never be enough for anyone.

"Cat got your tongue?"

She heaved a sigh. "I'm a workaholic. There just hasn't been time for romance."

One of his eyebrows rose in a charming

yet irritating way. "I'm sure the men in Camas, Washington, have tried, though."

She snorted and then clapped her hand over her mouth. Wow, so unladylike. Her mother would scold her good.

"Come on—you can't tell me you don't have men asking you out right and left."

"No, I don't." Though if he'd asked her out when she'd believed he was Wyatt Prescott, she'd have accepted. Bad on her for trusting the good-looking cowboy. Yet she was trusting her life to Jace's care. Ironic? Or plain dumb?

He pushed away from the tree. "Here's our bus."

Thankfully, they were done with the topic, and the constriction in her chest eased. They stepped in line to stow their bags in the underneath storage space before stepping onto the bus and handing over their tickets to the driver.

Jace led her to the back of the bus, in the emergency exit row. As they sat, he murmured in her ear, "Anyone who wouldn't want to ask you out is a fool."

His words created a storm within her that shouldn't be so full of pleasure. She scoffed. "Oh, come on."

He tucked in his chin, a gleam of something close to attraction flaring in his gaze, and a flushed heat rose in her cheeks.

"Darling," he drawled. "If you haven't looked in the mirror lately, you should. You're a beautiful woman with a smart mind. Any man worth his salt would be blessed to call you his."

Not quite sure what to do with his statement, she stared out the window and wished his words were true.

The big Greyhound bus rumbled down the freeway, passing the Texas landscape so familiar to Jace. He didn't take in the beauty of his home state. Instead, his mind kept replaying his own words.

Any man worth his salt would be blessed to call you his.

Why on earth had he voiced his attraction to Abby?

Not that his words weren't true. She was

beautiful and smart. And any man *would* be blessed to be included in her life.

Not him, though. At least, not in the way he suddenly longed to be. He couldn't put anyone through the turmoil of the long separations with no communication. The constant worry. He prayed he'd be able to keep Abby safe so she could have a normal life one day.

From beneath the brim of his hat, he noticed her eyelids flutter and close, and her head nod as sleep finally settled in. Gravity took over, and her chin came to rest on her chest. She was going to have a horrible crick in her neck when they arrived in San Antonio.

He shifted in his seat, putting his arm around her and easing her head gently to his shoulder. She gave a little sigh and burrowed closer. His heart thudded in his chest as tenderness filled him. What was he doing? Holding her like she was his? But she was his—to protect—and he couldn't stop the gnaw of worry in his gut.

What had happened to the real marshals

who were supposed to meet them at the airport? How had the cartel even known they were taking the JPATS? The questions rattled around in his head, making him anxious to talk to his father again. But every time he reached out to his father, he put everyone in jeopardy. Who was the mole within the Justice Department?

Against his shoulder, Abby let out a small noise that sounded suspiciously like distress. Hating that this ordeal had created nightmares for her, he tightened his hold and soothed a hand down her arm until she settled. Her sigh sent a ribbon of yearning through him.

Chastising himself for the attraction toward her simmering just beneath the surface, he reminded himself to stay professional and detached. A difficult task when he liked her determination and courageousness. From the first moment, she'd displayed an appealing strong inner core. If the situation were different— He cut the thought off. Best not to travel down a path of what-ifs. Those would only lead to disappointment and regret. He wasn't interested in anything long-term, no matter how appealing he found Abby.

By the time they arrived in San Antonio, his arm was numb, but he was loath to let go of her. He waited until everyone else had exited the bus before he gently nudged her. "Wake up, Abby. We're here."

She lifted her gaze to his, so adorably sleepy. "Hmm."

He traced circles on her shoulder. "Time to get off the bus."

She gave a little gasp of surprise and sat straight up, out of his grasp. Her cheeks pinkened. "Did I snore?"

He let out a chuckle, amused and charmed. "No. Maybe drooled a little."

Her eyes widened, and she wiped her mouth.

"I'm joking," he told her.

She wrinkled up her nose in such a cute way he had to fight the urge to kiss her. He abruptly stood, shaking out his numb arm as he shook off the totally inappropriate urge, and then helped her to stand. When they got off the bus and had collected their bags, he kept an alert eye out, searching for any kind of threat. He needed to find a phone so he could call his father. Fortunately, they weren't far from the River Walk. "This way."

He led her along a busy downtown road toward one of the many entrances that would drop them from street level down onto the crown jewel of San Antonio. The River Walk, named so because it followed along the winding path of water that bisected the city.

"This is magnificent," Abby said, her voice filled with awe.

"It truly is a marvel," he said, enjoying the delight lighting up her eyes as she took in the riverboats cruising along the waterway. "The River Walk stretches for fifteen miles and has many bridges crossing over it for pedestrians."

"I wish we had time to explore it."

Her wistful tone made something in his chest shift. He would love to show her the many places in the city where he'd grown up. The Alamo, the King William Historic District and the many other museums that had fascinated him as a kid. "Me, too."

He ducked them into a taqueria with outdoor seating. "A table for two. Near the water, if possible." A place where he could keep an eye on anyone approaching.

The hostess, a young woman with long dark hair in fancy braids, nodded and escorted them to a corner table beneath an umbrella where they had a nice view of the pathway and the riverboats floating by.

The hostess handed them menus, but before she could walk away, Jace asked, "Can I use your phone to make a local call?"

There was a brief hesitation before she shrugged. "Sure."

To Abby, Jace said, "I'll be right back."

Abby opened the menu. "I'll be here."

Jace followed the hostess to the entrance desk while staying alert for anyone who showed interest in Abby.

He hesitated before calling his father's work number. Using his father's work phone had brought the cartel on their heels on the way to the airport in Washington. Using his father's cell phone had landed them in hot water at the JPATS terminal in Austin.

He wasn't sure who to trust or which phone to call.

Opting for the emergency plan, Jace called his mother's landline. The family ranch was located on the outskirts of San Antonio and was in his maternal grandfather's name. Gavin Armstrong had insisted on distancing the family home from him as a precaution to keep his loved ones safe.

His mother answered on the second ring. "Hello?"

"It's a nice day in paradise," Jace said, using the secure phrase agreed upon years ago. Another of his father's safety measures.

"Indeed, it is." His mother's voice filled his ear. "Sunshine for days." Then she hung up.

Jace put the receiver of the restaurant's

phone back in its cradle and waited. Within seconds, the phone rang, and he picked up, ignoring the raised eyebrow of the hostess. "Taqueria La Bella."

He purposely said the wrong name of the restaurant just in case his mother's phone was being monitored. It wasn't likely, but he'd take caution over complacency any day.

"Jace, what's happening? Are you safe?" His mother's worried voice reached out to him, twisting his heart up.

"Hey, Mom. Yes, I'm safe. Can you call Dad and give him this number? But use your private phone."

His parents used a completely different cell phone and service to keep in contact. Jace never quite understood the importance of doing so until this very moment. He had never had to invoke reaching his father this way. Now he realized it was one of his father's safeguards, a way of communicating with his wife. A way not even Jace could access.

"On it." His mother hung up without preamble.

"Sir, are you and your friend going to order?" the hostess asked him.

Giving the young lady his best smile, he said, "Yes. Two sweet teas, chips and salsa to start."

The hostess blinked and gave a nod. She moved away to give a waiter the order.

The restaurant phone rang again, and he snatched the receiver up. "Taqueria La Bella."

"Jace."

Amazed at the relief washing through him at hearing his dad's voice again, Jace rattled off the address of the restaurant and hung up.

He gave the hostess a twenty-dollar bill. "Thank you."

She pocketed the money with a smile. "Anytime."

Jace returned to the table where Abby sat, her wary gaze taking in the crowd strolling up and down the River Walk. The sweet teas, salty chips and salsa he'd ordered were already on the table.

"My dad will be here soon. Until then, enjoy." He picked up his glass of sweet tea and held it out to her.

She smiled, took her glass and clinked it to his. She set the glass back down. "Why are you doing this?"

He sipped from the sweet concoction. "Doing what?"

"Constantly putting your life in jeopardy."

"It's what I do."

She considered his words for a moment and then nodded. "You're the wolf who keeps the sheep safe from those who want to harm them."

"I've never thought of it quite in those terms before, but okay." He liked the idea of being a wolf. Wolves had sharp teeth and were fast, yet stealthy. And a wolf would do whatever it took to keep his charges safe.

He reached out and took Abby's hand. A little frisson of sensation raced up his arm and settled near his heart. Both disconcerting and delightful. "I'm not going to let anything happen to you. You have to trust me on this."

Her gaze met his, and she covered his hand with her other hand. "Trust is not easily given. It has to be earned. You're doing a good job of it. I just want you to be honest with me. No more lies."

The insecurities and vulnerabilities deep in the depths of her pretty hazel eyes made his stomach sink. "Truth isn't always possible with what I do."

She removed her hands from his and gave a nod. "Then I suppose I must be content with only half trusting you."

SEVEN

Jace didn't like her pronouncement, but he had nothing to combat it with. He shook his head to dislodge the sadness and irritation vying for his attention. His mind turned to his mother, kept in the dark about his father's job. Jace had always known when she was sad or worried about his dad. It had filled Jace with dread and anger. They had gone long periods of time without any communication.

With a jolt, he realized he'd just proved his assumption as false. His mom and dad had always had a way to communicate. The emergency plan. It had been Jace who hadn't known how to contact his dad until he'd joined the marshals service. At that point, his father had told him if he ever needed to reach him to call the ranch and use the code words. A plan Jace had never had to use until now.

How much did his mother really know about his father's work over the years? Had his father confided in her? Kept her apprised of his whereabouts? How often had they employed the emergency plan? Ever?

Questions Jace would have to investigate when this was over. Though why he would, he wasn't sure. It wasn't like he had any intention of needing a plan of his own to keep the woman he loved safe while staying connected to her. He wasn't marrying, so it was a moot point.

"Why did my need to know the truth about my biological father push me into this?"

Abby's forlorn tone curled into his chest and brought his attention solely on her. "Curiosity isn't a bad thing."

She fanned herself with the menu. "My dad, the man who raised me, always said curiosity got the cat killed."

Jace couldn't stop a small smile. "But the cat had nine lives."

"Exactly." Abby's eyes grew big. "But whenever I said that to my father, he would say the cat didn't learn the lesson even though he had nine chances. The cat still died in the end."

"But the cat lived a full and adventurous life and was true to its nature."

She seemed to consider his words and then nodded. "Aren't you ever scared?"

The change of topic had him bouncing to keep up. "Of course. I'm human. But fear is an opportunity for us to utilize the courage residing in each of us."

Her eyebrows rose. "Sounds like a quote off a poster or something?"

He shrugged. "Heard it from my dad. I don't know where it came from. He probably made the saying up."

"Well, I don't know if I have any courage." She propped her elbow on the table and set her chin into her hand.

"Don't sell yourself short," he said gruffly. "You are one of the bravest women

I've ever met. Next to my mother. Most people would have never come on this journey. Most people would've sat home and let the curiosity eat away at them instead of chasing it down to find the truth."

Her troubled gaze met his. "But the truth could kill us."

"Hey, now." He reached out to gently smooth back a lock of her hair from her pretty face. "There's a big valley between will and might. And I choose to stay on the side of might. Besides, we've got God on our side, right?"

She closed her eyes and straightened her spine. "You're right. God is on our side." She stared out at the meandering river. "I hope I meet your mom one day."

He liked the idea of introducing them, but doing so also filled him with terror. What would taking her home to meet his mother signify?

Nothing more than he trusted Abby. "When this is all over, I will make sure you do."

Turning to face him, she met his gaze with a determined gleam. "When this is all over, I'll hold you to the promise."

Jace's heart bumped against his rib cage. A woman like Abby deserved more than he could ever give. And he never wanted a woman to be lonely and afraid, waiting for him and questioning if he was ever going to return home.

He gave himself a mental shake. Whoa, where were these considerations coming from? He'd let his guard down. His affection for Abby affected his judgment and *could* get them both killed.

Taking in the sights and sounds of the River Walk, Abby wished with everything in her this was just a vacation. A lark. That she was sitting in a cute little restaurant eating chips and salsa and drinking tea so sweet her teeth ached. She wanted to pretend this was a first date with the yummy cowboy appearing so at ease sitting across the table from her. But it wasn't a date.

She'd been around him long enough now to recognize how deceptive his body language could be. His gaze roamed the area, searching for a threat, and tension radiated off him in buffeting waves. He was a guardian. Protector. Her defense against the outside world. The barrier keeping her safe from the people who wanted to harm her.

As she dipped a chip into the pleasingly fresh salsa, she reminded herself there was a purpose for being here. She needed to discover the truth about Carlos Reyes and why someone was trying to either kill her or kidnap her. She also needed to keep from falling for Jace.

From beneath her lashes, she traced over his broad shoulders as he reached for a chip. She'd memorized the contours of him as she'd snuggled against him on the bus ride. Oh, how she'd enjoyed the scent of his aftershave and his masculinity. Heat crept up her neck. She couldn't believe she'd used Jace as a pillow. She had to admit she'd been aware of him pulling her close. The lure of sleep had been too strong, and her yearning to be close to him had been irresistible.

He'd made it clear a romantic relationship was not something he foresaw in his future. And having her heart broken wasn't on her to-do list.

Her gaze moved past Jace to a tall, lanky man striding through the restaurant. He was striking, with dark hair streaked with silver beneath a black cowboy hat and warm brown eyes. He wore casual cotton pants, a crisp white button-down shirt with a silver bolo tie and black cowboy boots. Her heart bumped against her ribs.

There was no mistaking the resemblance to Jace.

This had to be Gavin Armstrong.

She was right in her assumption. The man took the seat across from her, his gaze searching her face. "I can see your father in you."

His words caused a riot of emotions to

bubble up inside her. No one had ever claimed she resembled the man who'd raised her, Dan Frost. Anticipation of learning more about her biological father and dread that what she was about to hear would only end up hurting warred for dominance.

"Dad, this is Abigail Frost," Jace said. "Abby, my father, Gavin Armstrong."

Gavin extended his large hand, and she took it. He had the same calloused grip as Jace.

"Hello, Marshal Armstrong. Please, tell me about my father."

Gavin nodded, gave her hand a gentle squeeze and then released her. "I'll get to him." He turned to Jace. "Tell me more about the men who abducted you."

Abby swallowed back her impatience as Jace filled his father in on the details about the two fake marshals. "The one claiming to be George Jones had a very distinct scar on his face."

"I alerted the Austin office," Gavin said.

"They are searching for their marshals, and I'll update them with this info."

Heart aching, Abby lifted a silent prayer the real marshals would be found unharmed. She didn't want to acknowledge the reality they were likely dead. Because of her. Her throat tightened with guilt.

Gavin turned his focus to her, and she straightened, bracing herself for what he had to say.

"Carlos Reyes immigrated to the United States from Mexico when he was ten years old, along with his parents and an older sister," Gavin said. "When Carlos was eighteen, he took a job driving a transport truck. When he realized he was working for the Garcia Cartel, he abandoned the truck along a Texas highway and made his way north to Washington State. He met your mother two years later. But the cartel found Carlos and drew him back in."

Abby winced, because she suspected where the story was heading.

"One job, they told him," Gavin stated with a shake of his head. "Then they promised to let him go. Unfortunately, during the job, Carlos witnessed Marco Garcia, the son of the head of the Garcia Cartel, viciously kill a man."

Abby grimaced. Her heart hurt for Carlos.

"Carlos fled yet again, only this time he contacted the US Marshals Service. I was the marshal assigned to his case." Gavin ran a hand over his jaw. "Carlos was scheduled to enter WITSEC once he testified against Marco Garcia. However, he loved your mother enough to not want to drag her into the situation, so he convinced me to tell her he was dead." Sympathy flashed in Gavin's eyes. "He didn't know about you. If he had, things might've turned out differently."

Abby attempted to absorb the story with a sort of detachment in hopes it would let her process the words. But she couldn't detach enough to stop the deep ache throbbing beneath her breastbone. "He's alive, then."

"As far as I know, yes," Gavin said.

Something about his answer bothered her, but she couldn't place why. "Where is he?"

"I do not know."

She frowned, not believing him. The throb in her chest turned to an angry burn. "If he entered WITSEC, you do know where he is. You're choosing not to tell me."

Gavin exchanged a cryptic glance with his son.

Jace put his hand on Abby's arm, his touch tender and warm, caring. "Your father never went into the program. He ditched his protection detail and disappeared."

The words halted her breath. She searched Jace for any hint of duplicity. "You really have no idea where he is."

Gavin planted his hands on the table. "None."

Her gaze bounced between the two men. Father and son. US marshals. So much alike. "How did the Garcia family find out about me?"

Jace spoke again. "When your DNA connected to the Ramirez-Estevan family, it alerted the Garcia Cartel. We haven't quite figured out yet how this connects to Carlos. Your cousin Paulina is the key."

"But she didn't respond when I reached out to her."

"Paulina Ramirez-Estevan is eleven years old," Gavin said. "No doubt, an adult in her life discovered the connection to you."

"What?" This was all her fault. Heaps of guilt swamped her. Had she put this child in danger, too?

"How do you know this?"

"We have a dossier on the top people within the Garcia Cartel," Jace told her. "We know Edgar Estevan was a low-level minion who was killed in a car bombing several years ago."

Pangs of sympathy hit her. "Paulina's father?"

Jace and Gavin exchanged a glance.

"It's possible," Jace said. "Ramon Ramirez had been the right-hand man of Tomas Garcia, the head of the cartel. It's rumored he was killed by Marco Garcia, Tomas's son."

A shiver of fear whispered down her spine, a shudder following.

Jace smoothed his hand down her arm until his fingers wrapped around hers. Gratefully, she hung on to him. Even knowing she shouldn't rely on him, she couldn't help doing so. He was a steady presence keeping her from splintering into a thousand pieces.

Reeling from the revelations her biological father had once worked for a criminal cartel and had been targeted by those people made her realize how out of her depth she was.

The truth was worse than she'd ever imagined, yet it all made so much sense. The attempts on her life, the man demanding to know where Carlos was and now learning he had once been a part of a cartel. It was too much.

Now that she had the knowledge, all she wanted was to forget. She wanted to go back to her life and put this all behind her. She didn't want to meet Carlos or her cousin. She didn't want to stay in Texas any longer. "Thank you for telling me the truth. I'd like to go home now."

Silence met her announcement.

Jace gave her hand a squeeze. "Not a good idea."

Meeting his concerned gaze made the fine hairs on the back of her neck rise. "I don't care. It's my life. I want it back." She stared at Gavin. "Surely the US Marshals Service can put out some kind of notice to the cartel telling them I don't know anything. And convince them Carlos is deceased. He wants everyone to believe him dead, so let's believe it."

"It's not quite so simple," Gavin said.

Irritation mixed with dread jumbled up her tummy. "It has to be that simple." She rose, disentangling herself from Jace. "Make it happen. I'm going home."

Jace rose and captured her hand again, then tugged her back into the seat. "Take a breath. We need to strategize."

Gavin heaved a sigh. "Of course, we

can't keep you here against your will, Miss Frost. But the only way you are going back to Washington is with Jace in tow. You won't be safe until the cartel is convinced Carlos is gone for good. And there's no telling how long that will take."

She swallowed back the thrill and trepidation created by his words. Returning home meant Jace would continue to act as her bodyguard. Then what hope would she have of protecting her heart against him?

"Excuse me," Abby said as she rose. Jace ached at the distress on her lovely face. "I need to use the restroom. I'll be right back." She took her purse and hurried inside the restaurant.

Jace stood, intending to follow her, but his father stopped him.

"Give her a moment," Gavin said.

Tracking Abby weaving through the restaurant, Jace kept an alert eye for anyone else who might be interested in her. Several men's gazes followed her. Why wouldn't she turn men's heads? She was a beautiful woman. He studied each man, quickly deciding none posed a threat. There was no way the cartel could know they were here at this restaurant.

Frustration beat a steady rhythm against his breastbone as he resumed his seat. Abby was still in danger, and she wanted to return to Washington. He would have to return with her. To protect her. The notion of spending more time with her wasn't a burden. And he couldn't deny the thrum of anticipation reverberating through him. He clearly needed to get his head on straight.

After signaling to the waiter for their check, Jace turned his gaze to his father. "She and her family will need extended protection. We'll have to alert her place of employment, as well."

"Agreed." Gavin searched his son's face. "Are you sure you can be objective?"

Jace tucked in his chin even as his conscience waved a red flag. "What's that supposed to mean?"

"She's a beautiful woman, smart and interesting."

"What does that have to do with anything?" Jace hated the defensiveness in his tone. Apparently his father understood him too well. "I know my job. I'm really good at setting boundaries, Dad."

His dad made a face. "Too good, if you ask me."

Jace frowned. Wait. Wasn't his dad just warning him off falling for his protectee? "You're very confusing."

Gavin huffed out a sigh. "Just be careful."

"I'm always careful. I can only control so much." Guilt pinched him for the close calls Abby had already experienced while in his care.

"Believe me—I understand. But I'm not talking about the job. I'm talking about your heart."

Jace avoided his father's gaze and picked up his iced tea to drink the last of it. He'd rather avoid any conversation dealing with emotions. "No worries there."

"I'm not so sure."

Jace's gaze shot to his father. Heat crawled

up his neck at the intense scrutiny of his dad's gaze. "You don't believe I can handle this?"

"Oh, I know you can handle the job of protecting Miss Frost. And anyone else who comes along. But what I'm concerned about is Abby falling in love with you, and you're going to do what you always do. Bail. You're going to break her heart."

The words were like a stab to the chest. No way would Abby fall in love with him. She deserved somebody steady, someone serious and settled. Someone more like her. "You don't need to worry, Dad. Abby's smart. She won't fall for me."

"Son, if there's one thing I've learned in this life, it's that when it comes to the heart, intelligence doesn't always win."

Jace was saved from having to answer by the waiter coming with their check.

"I've got this." Gavin handed over more than enough cash.

When the waiter walked away, Gavin slid a set of car keys across the table to Jace. "I took one of the utility vehicles from the lot. No one knows I have it. It's untraceable. I'll make arrangements for you to get out of the state on a military transport. Head to Kelly Field. They'll know you're coming."

"How will you get back to the office?"

"I'll walk."

"Thanks, Dad. I appreciate it." He pocketed the keys.

Abby returned, her hair now in a braid over her shoulder. Her big hazel eyes met his, and she smiled tentatively. His heart did a somersault in his chest.

"What did I miss?"

Not about to tell her of their conversation concerning emotions and romance and hearts breaking, Jace said, "We're headed to the military base. Dad will arrange transport back to Washington."

As she slid into the chair, her gaze went to his father. "Thank you. You will keep us in the loop about whatever you find, correct?"

"I will, Miss Frost." Gavin patted her hand. "I will."

Gavin rose and pulled Jace into a hug, saying into his ear, "The vehicle is on the second deck of the parking garage, fourth stall in from the elevators."

Giving his father a squeeze, Jace said back, "You're the best."

"That's what they say." His dad grinned as he stepped away.

It was an old joke between them. There was comfort in the familiarity of it.

"You'll explain to Mom?" Jace said.

"Of course. There are no secrets between us."

Jace cocked his head at his father's words. Words he'd never heard his father utter. Words reminding Jace of his earlier questions about his parents. At some point, Jace would have to unpack the subject, but right now, his priority had to be guarding Abby.

As well as both of their hearts.

He prayed God would usher them safely to Abby's home.

They parted ways with his father, and Abby tucked her free hand around Jace's arm. With her other hand, she carried her overnight bag, and she had her purse across her body, while he had his duffel bag strap slung across his shoulder. Hopefully, they appeared to be tourists enjoying the beautiful fall day. He couldn't deny how nice it was to have her so close. Her lavender-and-vanilla scent teased his senses. A perfume as unique as the woman.

If this were a true vacation, or a date even, he would take her to the Alamo. Everyone who came to San Antonio should experience the Alamo and learn the history. But they weren't here for sightseeing. So instead, he steered her toward the parking structure for the Rivercenter mall. They found the unmarked black SUV easily enough. He unlocked the door and stowed their bags in the back. "Do you want to put your purse back here?"

"No, I'll hang on to it."

Once they were in the vehicle and heading away from the River Walk, Jace couldn't keep his curiosity in check. "What do you keep in that thing?"

From the corner of his eye, her quizzical gaze snagged his attention.

"Your purse," he clarified. "I've always wondered. Women seem to never want to be far from their purses. Like some kind of security blanket?"

She giggled. The sound was melodic and pleasing. "I've girlie things in here. You never know when you'll need them. Plus, I have an e-reader. Because you never know when you're going to be stuck somewhere and need to be entertained."

His gut clenched. She had an electronic device on her? "We need to get rid of it."

She gave a small gasp. "What? Could someone trace me through my e-reader?"

"It's not outside the realm of possibility."

Spying a garbage receptacle on the sidewalk, he pulled the vehicle to the curb. He placed the car in Park, turned off the engine and held out his hand. "Sorry, it's got to go."

Making a face, she dug through her purse and pulled out the square device.

He gripped the edge.

For a moment, she didn't let go. "Goodbye, little fella."

"Your e-reader is a guy?"

A pretty pink stained her cheeks. "I call it my book boyfriend. Because he holds all of my romance novels."

He grinned. "I didn't take you for the romance-novel type."

"I read across genres. Some of my favorite authors actually live here in Texas." She let go of the device.

"I imagine you have all of your books backed up somewhere?"

She made a scoffing noise. "Of course. Everyone knows to."

He jogged around the SUV to the sidewalk and dumped the e-reader into the garbage can. "'Bye, little fella."

Chuckling, he hurried back to the SUV, and soon they were on their way. To avoid rush-hour traffic on the freeway, Jace chose to take an alternative route. The windows were rolled down, allowing a warm breeze to circulate through the vehicle. Abby's vanilla-and-lavender scent swirled around him, filling his senses.

Suddenly, the SUV gave a lurch, and all the electronics, including the steering, gave out. His only course of action was to employ the emergency brake before he hit another car or pedestrian.

"What happened?" Abby clutched the door handle and the dashboard. Her wide-eyed gaze stared at him in alarm.

"I don't know." Distress invaded his stomach, crawling up his chest and into his throat. This wasn't good. Somebody must have used an electromagnetic-pulse device on the vehicle.

Even as the thought formed, several high-end SUVs with tinted windows screeched to a halt, surrounding them. Well-armed men wearing tactical gear jumped out.

The cartel had found them. Again.

EIGHT

Frustration burned in Jace's gut, and he reached for the onboard navigation system to send out a distress signal just as the doors of the marshals service SUV were yanked open. He froze.

A rough voice shouted, "Get out!"

"Jace?" Abby hesitated, alarm flashing across her pretty face. In her hand next to her thigh where the men outside the vehicle couldn't see it, she held a canister of pepper gel she'd tugged from her purse.

Breaking out in a cold sweat, Jace worked to keep his voice from reflecting the dread gripping him. There were too many of them for the gel to be of use. It would get her killed. "Drop that on the floor and do as they say."

Her brows dipped together, but she nodded, letting the canister fall to the floorboard, where it rolled beneath the seat. Then she slid out of the SUV.

Praying they lived through this, Jace hit the emergency alert button and climbed from the vehicle with his hands up. He elbowed the door shut as the emergency dispatcher's voice filled the interior. The last thing Jace needed was to let on he'd sent out an alarm. Help wouldn't arrive in time to save them, but at least the marshals service would be alerted to the situation.

The street was deserted, as if everyone in the area had gone to ground the second the cartel showed up.

A man rushed forward, relieving Jace of his weapon and pushing him toward the back passenger seat of one of the SUVs.

"No!" Abby's cry shuddered through Jace, and he broke away from his captor to rush to her side.

She clung to her purse with both hands as a thug attempted to take it from her.

Gently, Jace covered her hands with his. "It's not worth your life."

She dropped her purse on the ground with a defiant glare at the men.

"Hurry up. Get in." One of the thugs used the barrel of his gun to indicate they should climb into the vehicle.

They were being abducted. Better than being shot on the spot. But what destiny awaited them at their destination?

Once Jace and Abby were settled into the back passenger seat of the cartel's SUV, canvas bags were thrust over their heads. Jace gritted back his rising anger and reached blindly for Abby's hand. Her fingers curled around his and held on tightly.

He wished he could tell her not to worry, that everything would be all right, but he didn't have assurances to give. He had no clue how, or even if, they would survive this ordeal.

Words of faith played through his mind, bringing him as much solace as could be found, given the circumstances. Having escaped the fake marshals sent by the cartel, they'd still ended up in the clutches of Garcia's men. His gut twisted with dread. He'd failed to keep Abby from the long reach of the cartel. He didn't deserve to wear the badge.

After a long drive made excruciating by the canvas bag over his head, the SUV came to a halt. He mentally ran through where they might be, based on the time traveled—if they had gone south, which seemed the most likely, they could be near Laredo or Corpus Christi, or anywhere in between.

The bags were yanked from their heads. Jace blinked against the tempered glare of the afternoon sun shining through the tinted windows of the vehicle.

The vehicle's doors opened, and a man yelled, "Get out."

Mentally cataloging the men's descriptions so he could identify them later, Jace climbed from the SUV while tugging Abby to follow him. Once they were both on solid ground, she clutched the back of his shirt.

Jace took stock of their surroundings. The lush green landscaped gardens butted up against high stone walls. A way to keep the outside world from treading on the property. A huge sprawling house loomed in front of them, though the word *house* seemed like a misnomer considering the hacienda would take up a whole city block in San Antonio. More armed men dressed in tactical gear patrolled the grounds and the roof of the estate.

This had to be the Garcia Cartel's compound. They had been brought to the lair of the notorious drug kingpin.

"This way." One of the guards gestured with his automatic rifle toward the front entrance of the mansion.

Tucking Abby against his side and keeping an eye on the men with automatic weapons and sawed-off shotguns, he and Abby followed the guard up large stone stairs to a set of huge metal doors. The guard knocked twice. The doors opened slightly. The guard conferred with someone on the other side, and then the entrance was thrown open and they were ushered inside.

Luxury terra-cotta floors stretched through the entryway. Large oil and watercolor paintings of beautiful landscapes decorated the whitewashed walls. Bronze statues of various animals were showcased on pedestals. A curving wrought iron staircase led to a second and third floor.

"Move it."

The guard led them down the hallway past several closed doors and into a large den. Stopping in the middle of the room, Jace put a protective arm around Abby. Her body quivered beneath his touch, and she edged closer to him.

Floor-to-ceiling windows provided a view of a kidney-shaped pool, a wooden pool house and a set of tennis courts. Disdain for the display of illegally gained wealth burned in Jace's chest. The back area was cordoned off by a large full hedge the length of the property.

One wall of the office had bookshelves filled with leather-bound volumes. A large mahogany desk took up space in the corner; behind it sat the head of the Garcia drug cartel.

Tomas Garcia. He wore a bright short-sleeve shirt revealing tattoos on his biceps. He was stocky with muscles gone to seed, with a full gray head of hair. His obsidian eyes raked over Jace and Abby, making Jace's fingers curl with resentment. The man considered himself a king, untouchable and above the law. He'd managed for decades to evade arrest, and now, at seventy-nine, he had the gall to believe kidnapping a US marshal wouldn't bring his downfall.

Standing next to Tomas was his son Marco. Tall and wiry, there was little resemblance in stature to his father, but they had the same cold, hard eyes. Unlike his father, Marco dressed to impress in a well-tailored beige suit and gelled hair.

He could have walked out of an issue of *Fortune* magazine. The man appeared younger than fifty.

Jace swallowed back the trepidation threatening to rob him of breath. They were in the inner sanctum of the cartel. No way would these men let them live. As if sensing his grim thought, Abby pressed herself closer to him.

Going on the offensive, Jace faced the head of the cartel. "Why have you brought us here?"

"Deputy Armstrong, surely you aren't dense," Tomas said. "It's too bad it has come to this, but it couldn't be helped."

"You have nothing to gain by detaining us," Jace said. "Carlos Reyes is dead. Bringing us here is only going to make matters worse for you."

Tomas laughed. "Come now. You know that's not true. Your father is trying to find Carlos as we speak, so there must be some chance the man lives. I will send word to Marshal Armstrong, telling him he better hurry in his search for Carlos."

Beside him, Abby made a soft distressed noise. Jace tightened his hold on her. "Even if Carlos Reyes is alive, and I'm not saying he is, how do you know he will even care his daughter has been taken?"

Eyes sparking with anger, Tomas snapped, "He may not care about a daughter he never met, but I know your father will. And he will move heaven and earth to find you."

Jace's stomach dropped. What Tomas said was true. So now they were going to use Jace as leverage—his father's worst fear—to force him to bring Carlos to them. If his father could even find the man. "Then let Miss Frost go. She has nothing to do with this."

"Unfortunately, she has everything to do with this. She's Carlos's daughter and might be of use," Tomas said. "But we are not savages." He signaled to one of his lieutenants. "Take Miss Frost to a room upstairs and make her comfortable."

"No," Jace said. "We stay together."

Despite his protest, Abby was wrenched from his side.

"Jace!" Abby yelped. She stomped her heel on the guard's foot. "Let go of me."

The guard shoved her away from him with a growl of pain.

Another guard caught her, wrenching her arms behind her back and then quickly using zip ties to hold her wrists in place.

Jace growled and lunged after the guy manhandling Abby. Two other guards stepped forward and grabbed him, forcing him to just watch the guard lead a squirming Abby from the room.

Rage filled Jace's veins. He stared at Tomas. "You'll never get away with this."

"I already have." He gestured to his son. "Do what you will with him. Just keep him alive until we have Carlos."

The cruelty lighting Marco's flat eyes sent dread through Jace. Marco Garcia's penchant for violence was legendary, but at least Tomas had said to keep Jace alive. The command gave Jace hope there would still be a chance to escape. He had to save Abby. Somehow, someway, he had to get word out to his father. He had no idea how, though. In the meantime, he would endure whatever Marco had planned.

Marco gave a chin nod, and the two men holding Jace carted him away. As they led him back through the entryway, Jace's gaze went up the wide staircase. Abby was somewhere up there. Was she really safe? Would they harm her?

His gut churned, and he attempted to break free of his captors by twisting and headbutting one. The prongs of a Taser against his side momentarily rendered him immobile, his limbs stiffening and then going limp. He dropped to his knees, agony ripping through him.

"I'll keep it up if you don't cooperate," the guard ground out.

Jace debated his options as the men dragged him down a dark stairwell. He'd rather face the Taser than whatever unknown fate Marco had for him.

Abby was shoved into a beautifully appointed bedroom with a four-poster canopy bed. Large windows with frilly curtains overlooked the side yard. A writing desk sat in front of the window with a small chair. One of the guards cut the ties binding her hands, and then they silently retreated, leaving her alone. She rubbed at the sore spots on her wrists from the ties.

What would Jace do in this situation? Trying to channel him, she assessed her surroundings. There were two doors at the other end of the room. Quickly, she opened one door and found an empty closet. Not even hangers to use as a weapon. The second door opened to a marbled bathroom.

Hoping there would be something she could use to defend herself, she checked the drawers and the cupboards. All empty. She tried to lift the heavy porcelain lid off the toilet, because a blunt instrument was a blunt instrument, but it was somehow fastened down.

After abandoning the bathroom, she again searched the bedroom for anything useful to protect herself with but found only the small bedside table lamp and the delicate desk chair. Rubbing her arms against a sudden chill, she gazed out the window at the well-manicured lawn and lush foliage growing up a stone wall. The branches of a tree growing near the house caught her attention.

If she could break the glass and get to the tree, maybe she could escape. But what then? She couldn't leave Jace behind. Recalling the men with guns on the roof, she had no doubt she'd probably be dead before she reached the ground. Her stomach soured at the mental image.

The head of the Garcia Cartel wouldn't hesitate to kill her. They were using Jace as incentive for Gavin to find and bring Carlos here. Didn't these men understand? No one possessed information on how to reach Carlos. He could be truly dead.

She paced away from the window, her mind consumed with Jace's possible fate. What were they doing to him? How did they know Gavin Armstrong was searching for Carlos? They had to have somebody within Marshal Armstrong's office. But who had he trusted with the knowledge?

Turning her attention back to the problem before her, she weighed her options. What if she broke the window and then hid? The guards would assume she'd escaped. Then maybe she could find her way to wherever they had taken Jace.

Her skin prickled, and her heart thumped painfully in her chest.

Fear is an opportunity for us to utilize the courage residing in each of us.

Replaying Jace's statement bolstered her enough that she picked up the bedside table lamp and held it like a baseball bat. She took several breaths to steady her nerves. *Please, let this work!*

Bracing herself for flying glass, she swung the lamp at the window with all her might. Instead of shattering the glass, the lamp ricocheted off the windowpane like it had hit concrete, sending a reverberating pain through her arms and forcing her backward. She stumbled and landed on her backside with an oof.

Catching her breath, she gave a growl of frustration and threw the lamp across the room. It bounced on the carpet and came to a rest by the wall.

The windows were unbreakable. She pounded her fists on the floor, hating this helplessness stealing over her. How were they going to get out of this situation? She scooted back until she was leaning against the side of the bed. She bowed her head and did the only thing she could. She prayed.

Pain echoed through Jace's body with each precise and malicious blow Marco delivered. The crack of a rib and the ensuing biting agony had Jace clenching his teeth. No way would he give Marco the satisfaction of letting a bellow escape.

Jace's legs threatened to give out. His shoulders screamed in protest from bearing so much of his weight. The metal cuffs biting into his wrists were attached to a metal pipe built into the roof of the sparse utility room on the far side of a tricked-out game room.

Marco's thugs had dragged him down several flights of stairs to the basement that housed state-of-the-art electronic gaming consoles as well as a pool table, air hockey and a large-screen television with three rows of theater seats. They'd hauled him inside this concrete room and strung him up like a punching bag, chaining his hands over his head. Shortly after, Marco had shown up and viciously used Jace as an outlet for a clearly deep-seated rage.

Marco landed a right cross to Jace's chin, and his head snapped to the side. Blood pooled in his mouth, stars burst before his eyes and the world spun. Jace held on to consciousness by sheer force of will, his mind screaming with fear for Abby.

Jace closed his eyes, waiting for the next blow. When it didn't come, he opened his eyes and found Marco staring at him.

Marco's lip curled. "As much fun as this has been, I've work to do. I'll be back. We'll see how long you can hold out."

Growling, Jace wanted to wipe the smug expression off the man's face. Jace's body might break, but his will would never bend.

Marco's lips stretched in a grotesque smile. "I'll pay your lovely girlfriend a visit after I clean up."

Jace railed against the restraints. "You leave her alone!"

"Hmm, she means a great deal to you. Interesting. This will be fun." Marco turned and strode out of the room, wiping his hands on a towel.

If Marco laid one finger on her... Jace breathed through the anger and horror warring for dominance within him.

He held himself still. His shoulders ached, his feet barely touched to keep him upright. But if he gave in to rage by thrashing about, he might dislocate his shoulders and then he'd be no good to Abby if he managed to escape.

The door shut behind Marco, leaving one guard to stand watch. Jace stared at the guard. His gaze zeroed in on the ring of keys attached to the guard's belt. One of those keys had to be to the handcuffs holding Jace in place. He needed the guard to come close. Somehow, Jace had to get those keys.

Mumbling, Jace went on tiptoe to relieve some of the pressure in his shoulders. Continuing to mumble in hopes the guard would get curious enough to come closer, Jace subtly rolled his shoulder to alleviate some of the pain.

After a moment, the guard shouted, "Stop your bellyaching."

"Please." Jace infused his voice with entreaty. "I'm going to be sick."

"Then be sick."

There was no way the guard was going to get near. And even if Jace could somehow render him unconscious, he had no way to get the key and then get it to the chain over his head.

Despair engulfed him. Would he ever

see Abby again? He'd failed to protect her. He prayed God would spare Abby. She didn't deserve this.

Evening shadows grew long across the carpeted bedroom floor. Abby didn't know how long she had sat with her knees to her chest, using the bed as a backrest while she prayed. Stiffness in her joints made getting to her feet a chore. She retrieved the table lamp and was thankful the bulb hadn't broken when she'd thrown it across the room. She plugged it in and turned it on. A soft glow filled the space, its warming light belying the evil hidden in this home.

Noise outside the bedroom door sent her heart thumping. Were the guards coming to get her? For what purpose? She needed to be ready. She would not go down without a fight. She didn't know what they planned for her or for Jace.

Her stomach knotted. If he was even alive.

Grief and terror threatened to rob her

of rational thought, but she fought for clarity. Clinging to Jace's words that fear was an opportunity for courage, she dug deep within herself. She needed to be the bravest woman he'd ever met. Though she trembled inside, she picked up the desk lamp and yanked the plug from the socket, dousing the room in gloom.

Gripping the end with the intent of using the lamp base to bludgeon whoever walked through the door, she positioned herself near the doorjamb. She cocked her head to listen. A woman was talking to the guard.

Curious.

Suspending the lamp over her head, Abby held her breath as the doorknob turned and the door swung open. A woman stepped inside, silhouetted by the hall light. Her features were in shadow as she quickly shut the door behind her.

In the ambient light coming through the window, dark eyes collided with Abby. The woman's eyebrows rose, and her hands followed suit. "I'm here to help you," she said, her soft, melodic voice barely above a whisper.

Abby couldn't say why she hesitated to strike. "Who are you?"

The woman walked farther into the bedroom, her tea-length dress swirling around her like a white cloud in the evening light, and her dark curls cascaded down her back. She turned to face Abby, who stayed in the corner, lamp held like a bat, ready to swing.

The woman motioned her forward. "Come away from the door. I don't want the guard to hear."

Abby took tentative steps toward the woman, but she kept the lamp cocked over her shoulder. "What is going on?"

"I'm your cousin. From your biological father's side. My name is Inez Ramirez-Estevan."

Abby digested the words. "How do you know about me?"

Inez sighed. "I never dreamed my daughter Paulina's school project would result in this mess."

Paulina was the name of the person whose DNA Abby shared. The eleven-year-old girl was this woman's daughter. "Why should I believe you?"

"My mother, Dorcas Reyes Ramirez, is your father's sister. When my mother saw Paulina's family tree project...*guau*!" Inez shook her head. "I've never seen my mother so terrified. She confessed she had a baby brother Carlos Reyes. And you have to be his daughter."

Abby digested this info, which matched what Gavin had told her about Carlos's family. She lowered the lamp. "Why are you here in this place?"

"My mother married Tomas Garcia's top lieutenant, Roman Ramirez, my father. He died a few years ago. We've lived on this estate my whole life. Then I married one of Marco's lieutenants. But my husband died when my daughter was little."

Empathy twisted within Abby's chest. She tried to ignore it. She didn't want to sympathize with the people who were holding her and Jace captive.

"You have to believe me." Inez came forward to grasp Abby's free hand. "I had no idea my mother had a brother or that the Garcia family wanted him dead. They will do anything to complete their mission."

"I'm well aware of what the Garcia family is willing to do to find my father."

"Do you know where he is?"

Suspicions flared along with caution. Abby tugged her hand from the woman. Was Inez even telling her the truth? Or was this some elaborate scheme to try to trick her into telling the Garcias where to find Carlos? They would be disappointed.

"I don't know anything about Carlos Reyes. I just learned about him a few days ago. As far as I know, as far as the US Marshals Service knows, he is dead."

Inez stared at her for a long moment. "You truly believe he's deceased?"

The truth warred within Abby. Gavin's words haunted her. They weren't certain if Carlos was alive or not. He'd disappeared. But there was no way Abby would reveal what Gavin had told her. So instead of addressing Inez's statement, Abby asked, "What do you want with me?"

"I told you. I'm here to help you. I don't believe what they're doing is right. I can help you escape."

As much as Abby wanted to believe this woman, she couldn't shake the suspicion she was being set up. But to what end?

NINE

Abby stared at the woman claiming to be her cousin with distrust and caution. Did she dare believe her claim of wanting to help? "Why should I trust you?"

"What options do you have?" Inez countered.

The truth dug at Abby. Did she dare risk placing her life and Jace's in this woman's hands? The alternative was to do nothing. And that was unacceptable. "Do you know where they took Jace?"

A frown puckered Inez's forehead. "Is he the man you came with?"

"Yes. They took him away." From the maniacal gleam in Marco's eyes, Abby feared whatever the man had planned for

Jace was beyond horrible. "I can't leave here without him."

Inez shook her head, her dark curls swaying with the movement. "Trying to rescue him would be suicide. You need to save yourself. Get away and send back reinforcements."

Undoubtedly a wise plan, but everything inside her rebelled at the suggestion. Time and time again, Jace had put his life on the line for her. Yes, he'd been trained, and it was his job to protect, but she couldn't turn tail and run. Her conscience wouldn't allow it. "They'll kill him."

Inez cocked her head and narrowed her gaze. "Do you love this man?"

The question forced Abby back a step. "What? No. I barely know him."

The denial came quickly, but didn't ring true in her ears.

Did she love Jace?

She was grateful to him for saving her life multiple times. She cared about him. He was a good man. She worried he was hurt. Just the prospect of him suffering in any way had her stomach twisted like a pretzel. But love? She wouldn't let her mind, or heart, contemplate the emotion. There was too much at stake. Right now, her focus had to be on rescuing Jace and then escaping. Alive.

"You'd risk your own life for a man you barely know?" Inez's expression matched the doubt in her voice.

Debating her emotions for Jace wasn't productive. Abby needed to save him, despite the quiver of fear racing through her blood. "Do you know where they took him?"

With a sigh filled with resignation, Inez nodded. "I do. But getting to him will be difficult."

"Then we'll just have to brave the difficulty." And if she repeated the phrase enough, hopefully it would keep the terror at bay. "If you're sincere about helping me escape, then help me find Jace, so we can both leave here."

Inez was quiet for a moment. Then she took a deep breath and squared her shoulders. "All right. I would not be able to live with myself if I don't try to help you."

A sentiment Abby understood. Maybe they did share some of the same DNA.

Lowering her voice, Inez said, "We need to make a plan. And it needs to start with removing the guard from your door."

Abby dropped her voice to a whisper, as well. "If you'll lure him in here, I'll hit him over the head." She held up the lamp still clutched in her hands.

Inez eyed the makeshift bat. One corner of her mouth tipped up. "You're itching to do that, aren't you?"

"Frankly, I am." The admission surprised Abby. She didn't consider herself violent and wasn't sure she could go through with her threat to use the lamp as a weapon, but Jace's life was on the line. She needed to be strong and courageous.

"We don't want to kill him," Inez warned.

Abby recoiled. "Of course not. I'm not a killer." Abby bit her lip, hating to have placed another person in danger. "What happens when he comes to and tells them you helped me?"

"I'll say you had a weapon." Inez waved toward the door. "Take your place."

Abby hustled back to the corner behind the doorjamb, lifted the lamp over her head and prepared herself.

Then Inez called out, "Help! Help me!"

The door burst open. The guard rushed in with his automatic rifle sweeping the room. Inez held her hands up, her gaze meeting Abby with the clear message it was time to act.

Limbs shaking and barely able to take a full breath, Abby brought the lamp down on the back of the man's head. Shock waves from the impact reverberated up her arm. The guard staggered and fell forward, landing facedown on the carpet.

"Shut the door," Inez hissed.

Pushing the door shut, Abby placed the lamp on the floor. Her whole body quivered with adrenaline. She couldn't believe she'd just knocked somebody out.

Or worse. Her heart stalled. "Please, tell me he's not dead."

Inez checked his pulse. "He's alive. But we need to tie him up and push him under the bed."

They made quick work of using the lamp cord to bind the man's hands and feet. Abby ripped a piece of sheet from the bed and used it as a gag over the man's mouth. Inez grabbed the gun from him and pushed it to the side. Then they rolled him underneath the bed, as far into the deep shadows as they could.

Inez picked up the weapon. "Let's go."

Abby grabbed her arm. "Do you know how to use a gun?"

Inez shrugged. "Point and shoot?"

Choking back a strangled laugh, Abby managed to say, "Works for me."

Inez cracked the door open and peeked out. Abby, being several inches taller, peeked over her cousin's head.

Inez whispered, "The coast is clear."

They stepped into the hallway and shut the door behind them.

"This way." Instead of taking the main stairs down to the ground level, Inez directed Abby to another flight of stairs leading to an empty hallway near the kitchen. The sounds of food being prepared had Abby tensing.

Inez opened a door to yet another staircase leading down into yawning darkness. "Inside. Hurry."

Despite the hairs on the back of her neck rising in alarm, Abby took a breath and hurried down the staircase as quietly as she could. Inez followed her, shutting the door behind them and blocking out all the light.

Abby groped for the railing with one hand and reached for the next stair with her foot. Inez hovered close, urging Abby to move faster, but the fear of tripping forced Abby to a slower pace.

Finally, they made it to solid ground. Abby sensed they were in a cavernous space, and anxiety clawed up her throat. She'd never been bothered by the dark. Until now.

Inez used the flashlight mode on her cell phone to provide relief from the black abyss.

"You couldn't have used the light earlier?" Abby didn't try to hide her indignation.

"I wanted to make sure no one else was down here first."

A shiver of unease ran over Abby. The large space resembled the perfect frat house recreation room. "It's cold in here."

Inez ignored her and hurried to the far end of the long room and another closed door. Abby's heart pounded. Inez rapped lightly on the wooden door and stepped back. When the door swung open, allowing light to slice through the shadows, Abby swallowed as they faced another armed guard. The man was tall and imposing, with short dark hair and a close-cropped beard. A deep scowl was etched on his hard face.

"What are you doing here?" the man demanded in a hushed tone. His gaze shot to the darkness behind them and then back to Inez.

Inez stepped forward. "Miguel, let us in."

Miguel continued to block the entrance. "You're not supposed to be down here." His disdainful gaze flicked over Abby. "Neither is she. I don't understand. What are you thinking?"

Inez handed Abby the rifle she'd taken from the guard upstairs. Fumbling to hold the offending thing, Abby gaped as Inez placed her hand over the man's heart. There was definitely something romantic going on between these two.

"This is wrong, Miguel. You know it. She is my cousin. Family."

Abby sucked in a breath. Why would this man care?

Miguel's gaze bounced to Abby and then back to Inez. Indecision flashed in his eyes. "You don't know what you're asking."

"Yes, I do." Inez's voice softened. "You said you loved me."

Abby's mouth dropped open.

"And I know you love Paulina," Inez continued, referring to her daughter. "This isn't good for us. There's no way we will ever be able to be together as long as we're here under Tomas's thumb. You know this. Letting them go is our way out."

Miguel hesitated, but tenderness stole over his expression, softening the rock-hard plane of his face. He snaked an arm around Inez and kissed her.

Abby stared. She'd only witnessed kisses like that in movies. Embarrassment and a strange sort of longing washed over her.

From inside the room, someone groaned. Her heart jammed into her throat. Jace?

Miguel drew back from Inez. "I would do anything for you and Paulina. You know this. But what you are asking is madness. You'll get us all killed."

Done with waiting for Inez and Miguel to come to an agreement, Abby pushed past the pair. Inside the room, she came to an abrupt halt. Jace's hands were raised over his head and held fast by handcuffs and a chain wrapped around a pipe in the ceiling. His head hung forward, his chin resting on his bare chest. His knees had buckled, and the tops of his feet rested on the ground. Blood oozed from several gashes on his face and torso. Dark purple bruises marred his flesh.

A cry of anguish rose from deep within Abby. She set the rifle down and ran forward, placing her hands carefully on his battered face. "Jace."

One eye was swelled shut. The other eyelid fluttered open. He seemed to struggle to focus on her. "Abby? No! You shouldn't be here."

"Shush," Abby cooed. "We're going to get you out of here." She turned to Miguel and implored, "Please. Do you have the keys?"

With jerking movements, Miguel grabbed the key ring off his belt. He searched through the keys, chose one and thrust it at her.

There was no way she could reach the lock on the cuffs. "A little help, please?"

When Miguel hesitated, Inez said, *"Mi amor, por favor."*

Miguel growled. He stalked forward, slipped the key into the lock and released Jace. He crumpled to the ground.

Distressed, Abby knelt next to him and gathered him in her arms. "Jace, you have to wake up. You have to be strong enough to walk. I can't carry you out of here."

"And just how are *we* going to get out of here?" Miguel asked Inez.

"I'm sorry, *mi amor*," Inez said. "I'm going to have to knock you out. Then I will lead them through the garden tunnels."

Miguel glowered. "What? You said we were leaving together."

"We will. I promise. We can't leave with them. If Marco learns we helped them, we will never be safe. Paulina won't be safe." She wrapped her arms around Miguel. "We have to get them to safety so they can bring back the authorities. The only way we will ever be truly free is if Tomas and Marco are arrested and locked away."

Abby held her breath as Miguel remained silent.

Inez went on tiptoe and kissed Miguel. Abby turned away, uncomfortable to witness another display of affection between the two. She was even more discomforted by the yearning swelling within her chest. Her gaze collided with Jace's. He struggled to sit up, and she helped him as best she could.

He threaded a hand through her hair and pulled her closer. "I can't believe you're here."

Then his lips captured hers.

Abby melted into him as sensations rocketed through her. He tasted of salt and man and pain. She told herself to be mindful of his injuries, but he kissed her like she was special, and all reason left. She relished every second, not wanting the moment to end. The kiss was full of promise, full of hope. Her heart beat an erratic rhythm that had nothing to do with fear and everything to do with Jace.

A little voice inside her head cautioned

her not to read too much into this kiss. A kiss did not equal love or commitment. But it was a reminder they were alive, and for now, that had to be enough.

The clearing of a throat behind them broke them apart. Abby gasped for breath as she turned her gaze to Inez and Miguel.

"We need to go," Inez stated.

Abby turned to Jace. "Can you stand?"

"For you, anything." His lopsided grin made the swelling on his face more pronounced.

Abby's heart clenched, and his words burrowed in, making her ache in ways she didn't have time for. They needed to move, to escape. Shaking off her distress, Abby got Jace to his feet. His legs wobbled, and he leaned on her. She braced her feet apart to accept his weight and held on to him. It was her turn to be strong for him.

Miguel removed a small flashlight from a pocket and held it out to Abby. "You'll need this."

"Thank you," Abby said. She clutched the device in her hand.

He turned to Inez. "I'm ready."

Inez muttered what sounded like a prayer for forgiveness. Then she used the butt of the gun she'd taken off the upstairs guard and hit her beloved on the back of the head.

He staggered and crumpled to his knees, holding his head. "Go. I'll make it appear worse than it is."

"I'm sorry, my love." Inez kissed his forehead and then hurried to the door.

Abby and Jace hobbled after her. She took them through the recreation room and out a different door to a small garden with little lanterns providing splotches of light in the corners. A barely discernible water fountain gurgled nearby.

Inez pushed them up against the side of the house into the shadows. "Stay close to the wall. Up ahead there's a shrub concealing the entrance to a tunnel leading to town. It's roughly two miles. At the end, you'll come to a ladder and a trapdoor. You'll end up behind a cantina's garbage cans. Find the medical clinic. Tell Dr. Smithy I sent you."

Abby pulled Inez into a hug. "I can't thank you enough for this. Will you be all right?"

Giving her a squeeze before stepping back, Inez said, "I'll be fine. Everyone will assume you overpowered the guards and broke free."

"I pray you're right," Abby murmured. Though how anyone could believe those actions of her, she didn't know. She wasn't tough. She was just a banker from Washington.

"We need to go." Jace urged Abby forward.

They sneaked along the edge of the house, staying within the shadows until they reached the thick shrubbery. Just as Inez had claimed, there was a small gate hidden among the bushes. It swung soundlessly inward, allowing them access to a tunnel built of wood and dirt. Inside, darkness stretched endlessly. Jace stumbled, and she grasped him by the waist.

"Can you make it?"

"Yes," he hissed.

She shook her head, both grateful for his stubbornness and deploring it at the same time. Anyone would need a moment, or two, before going on the run after the beating he'd taken. After latching the gate, they moved slowly into the narrow carved-out passageway. She became aware of the earth beneath them sloping downward. She flicked on the flashlight. The round beam of light provided enough glow to illuminate two feet ahead of them. She could only guess the cartel used this as an escape route.

Something skittered along the floor in the dark. Abby halted and clutched Jace's arm while swinging the light back and forth. "Please, tell me there aren't rats down here."

"Rats are the least of our worries," Jace told her with wry amusement playing in his voice.

She couldn't argue with that fact. Still, she shuddered. "When I was a teenager, I went to church camp and found a rat inside my sleeping bag. He'd snagged a bag of chips and was eating them *in* my sleeping bag."

Jace chuckled. "I will protect you from any rats."

Keeping an arm around him, Abby sent up prayers for safety and stamina as they proceeded farther into the long tunnel.

Jace hissed in a breath, trying desperately not to alert Abby to the fire licking along every single one of his nerve endings. From the moment he'd regained consciousness and his vision had cleared enough for Abby's dear sweet face to come into focus, Jace had thanked God for giving him a second chance to protect her.

Kissing her had been instinctual.

An affirmation of life.

A silent acknowledgment that he'd despaired he'd never be with her again. The possible reality had been more torturous than the pounding of Marco's fists. Despite Jace's best efforts, he was becoming emotionally attached to this woman, and he had no clue what to do about it.

It had taken every ounce of strength he had to get himself to his feet. He'd tried not to lean too heavily on Abby for fear he would crush her, but he'd needed her help. Still did as they stumbled through the narrow passageway.

Though the flashlight Abby held illuminated the two feet in front of them, he occasionally rammed into a wooden beam. Each time set off another round of sparkling fireworks of pain through his system. He prayed Abby didn't realize just how badly he was injured.

"Can we stop for a moment?" she asked, forcing him to lean against the tunnel's dirt wall.

He acquiesced even though he realized she was taking the break for his sake. His head throbbed and his body ached. Her apple scent was a welcome relief from the musty smell of the tunnel. Though he couldn't see her in the dark, her face was imprinted in his mind.

After several long minutes, Abby tugged on him. "We have to keep going."

As he pushed away from the wall, a wave of dizziness washed over him. He couldn't get his bearings. Were they still headed in the right direction?

At Abby's urging, they continued trudging through the dark. He had to trust she had a better sense of direction than he currently possessed. The longer he stayed upright, the harder it was to remain standing. With gritted teeth, he forced himself to keep putting one foot in front of the other. Sweat broke out over his body. He shivered.

Abby tightened her hold on him. "You've got this. You can do it."

Her encouragement meant more to him than he could have expressed. He clenched his jaw and dug deep for every ounce of strength. Time passed, but how long, he couldn't have said.

They reached the end of the tunnel and stopped at the base of a metal ladder. He flexed his fingers, praying for the strength to make it up through the opening. "I'll go first. To make sure it's safe."

"I'll be right behind you," she muttered.

With grim determination, he grasped the rung and then inch by excoriating inch, he lifted himself up the ladder until he reached the trapdoor. He tested the door and breathed a sigh of relief when it cracked open.

Using his good eye, he peered through the opening. Moonlight provided enough luminosity for two large dumpsters to be visible. Music and laughter drifted on the night air from the cantina Inez had mentioned.

With effort, he climbed out of the tunnel, caution bracing his muscles. In a crouch, he held the door open and glanced around. No one was about.

Abby was up the ladder and climbing through the opening before he could offer her help.

"Clever," he said as he soundlessly closed the trapdoor. The edges of the door blended into the wooden slats of the platform holding several large metal garbage containers.

It would be nearly impossible to discern unless one was searching for it.

"We made it," Abby breathed.

"We still have a long way to go before we're safe," Jace whispered. "We don't know if this town is loyal to Garcia."

TEN

Jace squatted down with his back resting against the wall of the cantina. His energy seeped into the ground. Unfortunately, they had to keep moving. Soon, it would be daylight and they would be exposed. He had no doubt there would be people on Garcia's payroll in this town. No doubt, Garcia used the tunnel as a private route in and out of his estate.

Jace took a couple of breaths, which hurt as the broken ribs dug into his cartilage and muscles, but at least he could breathe. He didn't have a punctured lung.

Abby's gentle touch startled him. Her hand caressed his shoulder and moved tenderly to his face. "I can only imagine how hard this is for you physically."

As tempting as it was to nuzzle into her touch, he dug deep, getting his feet under him and his temptations under control. "We need to keep moving. No time for me to indulge in self-pity. Besides, I've been kicked by a horse. This isn't even as bad."

She let out a small huff. "It's not self-pity for you to take a moment. You're injured. I can't believe you're still upright."

For some reason, the edge to her voice made him smile. His little warrior. Did she even realize how strong and brave and courageous she was? How much he appreciated those traits? How much he was coming to care for her?

No. She didn't know what was in his heart, and he'd just as soon keep her unaware. There was no reason to muddle the situation with unwarranted emotions.

"I'll take a moment once we're safe."

"You're a stubborn man."

"I am." He couldn't keep from threading his fingers around hers and pressing their palms together. "Let's find the medical clinic."

Every step shot white agony through his body, making his head throb and his vision swim. But he gritted his teeth and ushered her into the shadows of the buildings lining the street.

A man stumbled out of the cantina and leaned against the pole holding up the awning over the entrance.

Freezing in place, Jace turned so his body hid Abby. He sent up a prayer the man wouldn't notice them only five feet away. Placing a hand on the building, he leaned in, nuzzled Abby's neck and wished they were somewhere else where they were free to explore the zing of attraction making his pulse pound.

After a long heartbeat, the man pushed away from the pole and staggered down the street.

Moving away from Abby required more effort than it should have. Jace tugged her in the opposite direction. "We need to find a phone."

"Yes. And we need to get you medical attention. There's the medical clinic,"

Abby whispered. "See the sign over the door?"

Blinking, he tried to focus, but the words blurred. "I'll take your word for it."

"Good." Abby wrapped an arm around his waist and urged him forward.

They tried the front door. Locked. Not unexpected so early in the morning. He leaned against the stucco wall, willing himself to keep putting one foot in front of the other. His feet were heavy as if encased in cement bricks. They moved silently around to the back door. Also locked.

Abby broke away from him to check the windows. "Jace, over here."

Her whispered call drew him to the far side of the building. A window had been cracked open. It was too high for Abby to reach. There was no help for it. Jace was going to have to give her a boost. He pressed his back to the wall, using it for support, and braced his legs apart. With slow, measured movements, he crouched, setting off a raging inferno of pain speeding through his veins and along his nerve endings. He gritted his teeth but managed to say, "Use my thigh as a step. I'll lift you up."

"Are you sure?"

Though the inky darkness hid her face from view, the worry in her tone was unmistakable. Impotent rage twisted in his chest. He couldn't make this better for her.

"Do it," he ground out.

Bracing her hands on his shoulders, she stepped onto his flexed thigh and reached upward for the window. "I've got the ledge. Can you get me a little higher?"

Sucking in a sharp breath of agony, he grasped her by the waist and used the last of his strength to lift her farther. She scrambled through the window, relieving him of her weight, and he sank to the ground, breathing hard as if he'd sprinted a fifty-yard dash. He clutched his side where Marco had viciously used him as a punching bag.

The world tilted. No. It was him tilting, slowly falling sideways.

Then Abby was there, her cool touch on his face, and her lips pressing against his brow. He wanted to revel in her touch, but unconsciousness threatened.

"You're feverish."

The alarm in her voice sank into him. He didn't want to distress her, but he couldn't form words.

She grabbed his shoulders, tugging and pushing until she was under his arm and lifting him upright. He hissed as another wave of pain shot through him.

She stilled. Her breath fanned over his face. "Jace, just a little bit more," she said into his ear. "I need you to be strong. Let's get you inside."

He would do anything for her. Walk through fire, take a bullet, whatever it took. The realization left him almost as breathless as the riot of agony twisting through every fiber of his being.

Sending a prayer upward for enough power to move, Jace maneuvered his legs beneath him, once again using the wall as leverage.

"Lean on me," she instructed.

There was no way she could take his full weight. He'd crush her. His legs wobbled, requiring him to give her some of his weight. She practically dragged him to the back door of the clinic, where it stood open.

Inside the building, she directed him to a couch in what was probably the waiting area. He sank down onto the cool leather cushions and stretched out. He let out a sigh as some of the pressure relented, but he couldn't stop from going under into the blessed oblivion of unconsciousness even as guilt for leaving her unprotected stabbed him in the heart.

Distress danced along Abby's nerves. Jace lost consciousness sprawled out on the couch. She was amazed he'd made it this far. He was a remarkable man. Her heart thumped as a riot of emotions clamored for attention. But now was not the time to analyze her reactions to Jace. She took a step back, both physically and emotionally.

She needed to focus on getting his fever down and relieving his pain, then calling the marshals. Worrying about whether she was falling for him or not was a moot point. He didn't want a wife or family. But their kiss lingered in her mind like a sweet treat. And she wanted more. The way he'd burrowed into her neck, protecting her from the view of the man who'd stumbled out of the cantina, made her skin prickle with longing.

With a shake of her head to dislodge the memory, she set out to find medicine to help Jace.

Loath to turn on the light or use her flashlight and announce their presence, she navigated her way through the medical clinic, which was like traversing an obstacle course. She bumped into a chair. A table. A cabinet that rattled. Each noise sent panic jolting through her veins, and she prayed there was nobody living upstairs.

She found the exam room. A locked cabinet held various drugs. There was a desk in the corner. She opened the drawers and found a bottle of over-the-counter pain reliever. This would at least help. She bumped her way into what appeared to be a small kitchen. Light eked through the window over the sink as the first rays of sunrise broke over the horizon. Daylight brought more danger.

Best not to borrow trouble prematurely.

She was grateful to see there were cases of bottled water stacked in the corner of the kitchen. She opened the top case and grabbed two bottles. There was a small refrigerator, and she cracked open the freezer on top and breathed a sigh of thanks when she found ice packs. She grabbed two of them and hurried back to Jace's side. She put one of the ice packs under his neck and the other on his forehead, just like her mother would do when she had a fever as a child. She cracked open both bottles of water. She drank from one and set it aside.

Gently, she shook Jace. "Come on, Jace. You need to wake up for a moment. Just long enough to take some pain meds."

He moaned. She took the noise as a good sign. She shook him again. "Jace, darling, please. Wake up."

The grip of unconsciousness had him too deep. She didn't know what to do. She tried lifting his head to give him a drink of water, but the liquid ran out the sides of his mouth. Afraid she'd choked him, she stopped. Bowing her head, she whispered, "Dear Lord, please, help me to help Jace. I don't know what to do here."

She had to find a phone. But did she dare call the marshals service? Would the mole inside the department send Garcia's men? Did she dare call 911?

The sudden creak of floorboards overhead sent a cascade of fear zipping along her nerves. A light came on at the end of the long hall, revealing a staircase. She sucked in a sharp breath. Panic reared, making her scramble to her feet. She had to protect Jace, but how? She had no weapons.

A gray-haired man with a gray beard shuffled down the stairs in a long night-shirt. He spoke in rapid Spanish and Abby couldn't translate quickly enough to understand.

Fighting the waves of terror clogging her throat, Abby fought to maintain her composure.

The old man turned on another light, reaching Abby and Jace with its warm glow. Viewing Jace fully in the light had her breath catching. His skin was so pale where there weren't black-and-blue bruises.

The man halted, his hands coming up as if she held a gun aimed at him. His eyes widened. Again, he spoke in rapid Spanish.

"Do you speak English?" Her voice wobbled.

"Of course. Who are you? What do you want?"

"Are you Dr. Smithy?"

Wariness gathered on his lined face. "I am."

Another measure of her tension was released through a noisy breath. "My cousin, Inez, told me to find you. My friend needs help."

"Inez is your cousin?" Doubt laced his voice. "She's never mentioned a cousin when she was here volunteering."

"It's complicated. Please, we need your help." She couldn't keep the entreaty from her tone. "We aren't here to harm you. We just want to go home. If you have a phone, I will call for someone to come get us. Please, he's burning up."

Lowering his hands, the man shuffled forward. "All right. For Inez, I will help you. Let's see to your man. Then you can use the phone."

The doctor examined Jace. "He most likely has cracked or broken ribs. We must call for an ambulance."

"No!" Abby swallowed back the trepidation threatening to rob her of sense. "Please, no one must know we're here. Inez said we could trust you."

Dr. Smithy frowned. "I'll do what I can for him."

"Thank you." She sent up more prayers for Jace's healing.

The doctor went into the clinic room and returned with a wide elastic bandage, a syringe and a vial.

Abby stood by as the doctor wrapped Jace's ribs. Then the doctor filled the syringe from the vial.

Concern arced through her. "What are you giving him?"

"Antibiotics for the fever. And some pain medication."

He gave Jace a shot and then moved away.

Abby knelt on the floor next to Jace's prone body. She took his hand in hers and kissed his knuckles. "Please, survive. Please, don't die on me." Her heart couldn't fathom the idea of him dying because of her.

Aware of the doctor's gaze, she glanced at him. "Do you have more ice packs?"

The doctor nodded. He disappeared and came back a few moments later with fresh ice packs. He quickly changed out the two ice packs she'd already used.

Her stomach grumbled loudly, and heat flushed through her face.

"When was the last time you ate?" Dr. Smithy asked.

"Sometime yesterday."

"I'll make you some food."

Though she needed to keep up her strength for both her and Jace, food wasn't a priority. "Can I use a phone?"

Dr. Smithy nodded, turned and went back upstairs. She sent up a little prayer, hoping he wasn't reaching out to the Garcia Cartel. But what choice did she and Jace have at this moment? None. They had to trust the older man. They had to trust God.

Holding on to Jace's hand, she leaned

against the couch cushion and fought to keep her eyes open, but the drowsiness overwhelmed her. Her eyelids grew heavy. It would be okay to close her eyes for just a moment.

The smell of eggs alerted her of Dr. Smithy's presence seconds before the clearing of a throat. She opened her eyes to find the doctor, who'd changed into dark pants and a long-sleeve button-down shirt, placing a plate of fluffy eggs and a fork on the table in front of her, along with a cell phone.

Shaking off the drowsiness, she released Jace's hand and met Dr. Smithy's gaze. "Thank you again. Can you tell me where we are?"

Dr. Smithy's eyebrows slammed together. "Oilton."

She didn't know Texas, so the name had no meaning to her. The doctor must have sensed her agitation, because he said, "We're about forty minutes from Laredo."

The name of a town she recognized.

"Great. I don't know how we will repay you."

"By leaving as soon as possible. I have patients coming this morning." He walked away.

Despairing of how she was going to get Jace somewhere safe, she ate quickly while the food was hot, thankful for the nourishment.

Staring at the phone, she weighed the risk of calling the marshals service and concluded the call was worth it. She quickly searched the cell phone's browser for the Laredo US Marshals office's phone number and then pressed the number to connect the call. Within seconds, a male voice answered, "US Marshals Service Laredo."

"I need to get a message to Marshal Armstrong in San Antonio," she said.

"Your name?"

Hesitating for fear her name would alert the mole inside the Justice Department, she took a moment to formulate what to say. "Mrs. Prescott. Please, tell Marshal Armstrong that Mr. and Mrs. Wyatt Prescott need his help. It's a matter of life and death." Surely evoking the name of Jace's undercover ID would hasten his father to return the call.

"Mrs. Prescott, will Marshal Armstrong be able to reach you at the number you're calling from?"

Not surprised the marshals office had the ability to capture the incoming call's phone number, she said, "Yes. Thank you." Her hands were shaking as she hung up. *Please, Lord, I hope I made the right decision.*

She rose, then took her plate to the kitchen, where she found Dr. Smithy. "I'll need to hang on to this phone. I'm waiting for a call."

He contemplated her for a moment. "I figured as much."

"We'll be gone soon." At least, she hoped and prayed so.

Appearing troubled, the doctor said, "Your man is in no condition to travel."

Her shoulders sagged as his words took

root. A part of her wished she could claim Jace as hers.

"We'll have to move him upstairs, though," the doctor said.

Her gaze went to the steep staircase. How on earth was she going to get him up the steps by herself?

As if reading her thoughts, Dr. Smithy said, "I'll take one side, you take the other. We must risk moving him. You can't be found here. People will notice a man in his condition. Word travels fast and could have dire consequences. I'm sure you agree."

At his meaningful stare, she nodded. Apparently, the doctor didn't want to bring the wrath of the Garcias down on him, either.

Working together, they managed to get Jace upright. Dr. Smithy took most of Jace's weight.

"What...what's happening?" Jace mumbled, his voice thick with agony.

"We have to move you," she told him.

"You have to be strong again. You can do this."

By the time she and Dr. Smithy got Jace to the top of the stairs, she was sweating, and her limbs were shaking from exertion, but she held on to Jace with all her strength as Dr. Smithy led them to what appeared to be a guest bedroom. They laid him on the bed, and she gently tugged Jace's dirty shoes off before lifting his feet to let him stretch out on the sheets.

"I'll bring fresh ice packs." Dr. Smithy left, closing the door behind him.

Abby sat beside Jace, pulled the light-weight cover over him and worked to calm her racing heart. The rising sun filtered through the curtains with long fingers of light. She glanced at the phone in her hand, willing it to ring.

Dr. Smithy returned and placed an ice pack once again beneath Jace's neck and one on his forehead. He patted Abby's shoulder. "You should rest, too. There's nothing more to be done now."

"Thank you again."

At the door, Dr. Smithy paused. "Please, keep quiet."

Abby nodded as her stomach clenched with dread. Discovery could mean their deaths.

She moved to the overstuffed chair in the corner and curled her feet beneath her. As she hovered on the edges of sleep, she prayed God would heal Jace and save them from this dire situation.

Sometime later, Abby awoke with a start. Heat from the sun made the room claustrophobic. Fanning herself, she glanced at the phone. No missed calls. She let out a soft growl of frustration.

Noises from outside and from the medical clinic below where she and Jace were hiding had her nerves jumping. She uncurled from the chair in the corner with a quick glance at Jace, verifying he was still unconscious. Cautiously, she moved to the window and pushed the curtain aside a smidgen so she could peek out.

Her breath caught in her throat. Two black SUVs, like the one that had brought them to the Garcia estate, were parked out front. At least a dozen of Garcia's men flooded the street. One of them was the man with the scar who had posed as a fake marshal. Panic flared like a scorching breath across Abby's nape. They were about to be discovered.

Another man with a bandage wrapped around his head climbed from the vehicle and turned slowly toward the medical clinic. Abby sucked in a breath. Miguel.

Questions raced through her mind. Was Inez okay? Had Garcia's men bought the story of her and Jace overpowering the guards to escape?

Miguel's gaze raked over the building. For a split second, his gaze collided with Abby's. She shrank back, letting the curtain fall closed. Her pulse pounded in her ears. Would he give them away?

She raced to the door and turned the lock, even though the flimsy mechanism would be no match for the men hunting them.

She searched the room for something to

use as a weapon but found nothing that would be effective against the cartel's army. She stilled as a commotion of angry voices downstairs had her heart jamming into her throat. The clopping of heavy feet coming up the stairs set loose a surge of terror.

Wishing she had a weapon, she backed toward the bed, putting herself between the door and Jace. Her gaze flew to the bedside table lamp, but there was no time to grab it.

The door burst open with one kick. Miguel filled the door frame, his dark eyes narrowed, his mouth set in a grim line.

Abby opened her mouth to beg him not to hurt them, but he put a finger to his lips.

Heart hammering in triple time, Abby nodded and mouthed, "Inez?"

Miguel gave her the okay signal with his hand.

A voice from the bottom of the stairs shouted up, "Miguel?"

"Nothing up here," Miguel called back to the unseen man before backing out of the room and pulling the door closed, though it couldn't latch.

Abby sank to the floor and stifled a sob of relief.

Jace groaned, the sound as earsplitting to Abby as a gunshot blast.

Abby scrambled to her feet and hurried to his side. "Shhhh."

She had to settle him before the cartel discovered Miguel's duplicity and came for her and Jace.

ELEVEN

The first thing Jace noticed as consciousness returned was the dull throbbing ache throughout his body. Where was he? What had happened?

Memory returned like a sledgehammer to his brain. He and Abby had escaped the Garcia Cartel compound through an underground tunnel and had come up through a trapdoor in a small town. They'd found the medical clinic Inez had told them to go to, but everything after was a blank. On a breath that shuddered through his limbs like an earthquake, he opened his eyes. Bright light stung his retinas. He blinked, attempting to focus. Where was Abby?

A piercing jolt of alarm rocketed through him.

The bed dipped, causing another riot of pain. And then she was in his view.

Relief made his limbs languid.

She used a cool, wet cloth to touch his face, wiping his cheeks and his neck. Tension eased, releasing some of the agony into the soft mattress beneath him.

"I'm so glad you are awake." Her smile was brighter than the sunlight filtering through the curtained window.

His heart seized. He opened his mouth to speak, but only a dry croak came from his parched throat.

"Hold on," she said, slipping out of view. And then she was back, one capable hand lifting his head while the other brought a small cup of water to his lips. The cool liquid slid down his throat and made him moan with relief.

"Slowly. You don't want the water to come back up."

He forced himself to measure his intake.

The water rinsed the dryness from his mouth and throat. He nodded to indicate he was done, and she took the cup away.

"What happened?" he asked.

"You ended up with a fever. Dr. Smithy has been giving you antibiotics. The fever broke early this morning."

"How long?"

"Twenty hours."

The words echoed through his head. She'd been unprotected and at the mercy of the Garcia Cartel for nearly a day! How could he have let this happen? His father never would have let something like this happen.

His father. Jace winced, knowing his dad would be beside himself with worry. And his mother, too. Jace tried to sit up, but a sharp tingling pain made him reconsider moving.

"You have two broken ribs. And the doctor says probably a bruised spleen, but only tests run in a hospital will confirm."

"No hospital. That would be the first place the cartel would search."

"I figured as much. You need to take it easy and regain your strength before we move you again."

A raw helplessness stole over him, making his voice sharp. "Are we safe?"

"We are. The cartel came hunting. But Miguel protected us."

As she told him about nearly being discovered, his heart rate ticked up. Thank the Lord above they'd been spared. For now. "We need help. I have to let my father know we're alive."

"I called the Laredo marshals office and asked them to get word to your father that Mr. and Mrs. Wyatt Prescott needed his help," she told him.

Clever of her to use his alias to signal his father they were in trouble. "Did he call back?"

She shook her head, her pretty gaze concerned. "I wasn't sure if I should call the San Antonio office or not, what with the mole inside the department."

His gut churned. She'd been right to hesitate. They couldn't reach his father through the normal channels. Someone within the US Marshals Service was feeding the cartel intel. But who? And why hadn't his father returned the call? Had someone in the office intercepted the message?

Or had something happened to his father? The possibility threatened to reduce him to a quivering mess. He had to do something.

"I'll call my friend Brian. I trust him. He'll come." Deputy US marshal Brian Forrester had worked out of the Los Angeles office for the past year, and they had grown close during training. "Where are we?"

"Oilton. Outside of Laredo." Abby rose. "The phone's downstairs charging. I'll be right back."

She left the room, then closed the door softly behind her. No way was Jace going to just sit idly by awaiting the next threat. Vulnerability fit like shoes two sizes too small. He refused to be helpless. Sucking in a steadying breath, he pushed himself up into a sitting position. Sweat broke out across his body. His frame quaked and his stomach roiled. Breathing as if he'd run a race, he stayed still until the worst of the nausea passed.

He grabbed one leg by the knee and lifted it over the side of the bed. The movement sent another wave of nausea and agony zipping through him. He grabbed his other knee, forced the leg to join the first one and scooted to the edge of the bed. Dizziness caused the room to swim. He clamped his teeth together to keep the meager contents of his stomach locked inside. He clenched his fists and waited, focusing on a spot on the wall with a faded outline where at one time a picture had hung. He was still waiting for the dizziness and nausea to pass when Abby opened the door.

She gave a little gasp and ran to him. "What do you think you're doing?"

The stern tone of her voice made him want to smile, but the effort was beyond him. She grabbed him by the shoulders and crouched until she was in his face, filling his vision with her beautiful eyes and the worry lines he'd put there.

"You need to lie down and rest," she admonished.

"Food?" he managed to say, though the idea of anything hitting his stomach brought on another wave of sickness. But he had to regain his strength. If he could eat, he could mend.

She pressed her lips together and concern flashed in those beautiful eyes.

"I'll get you some food if you'll lie back against the headboard."

Unwilling to admit the idea sounded like the best option, because he was afraid if he tried to stand he'd just collapse again, he agreed. "Deal."

She did something with the pillows and urged him to scoot back toward the wooden headboard. Fiery pain, like a live electrical current, licked along his limbs. Hitching his breath, he pushed his hips toward the headboard until he was able to rest his back and neck against the soft pillows. The air swooshed out of his lungs as she lifted his legs and gently swung them back onto the bed. He couldn't stop the moan of agony from escaping.

Her gaze shot to his. "I'll get the doctor."

He reached for her, grasped her wrist and slid his hand to hers, where he entwined their fingers. He tugged her closer and drew her hand to his lips to place light kisses on her knuckles. His gaze remained riveted to hers.

Her eyes widened. Her breath quickened. So pretty. The urge to kiss her was strong.

"Thank you," he murmured, as tender affection rose within his chest and chased away the throbbing pain. "I probably would've died if not for you."

Her gaze narrowed. "You better not die on me, Jace Armstrong. Ever."

The words hit him like a splash of cold water. "That's not something I can ever guarantee, darling." He let his drawl thicken to hide the effect of her words.

An emotion he couldn't name flashed

across her face. Too close to sadness and despair for his liking.

"I know," she said softly. "You're a man of action with a job that puts you in the line of fire. Believe me, I could never forget."

Neither could he. But he didn't want her to expend her energy worrying about him. He wanted to focus on her. "You're brave, courageous and beautiful. And I—"

He what? Wanted to declare his undying love?

His gut tightened. He couldn't. He could never subject anyone, especially this fascinating and admirable woman, to the sort of constant stress his mother had endured. To be alone for long periods of time while Jace worked at a job he couldn't discuss. Never knowing if he'd return.

"I'm grateful," he managed to say around the lump forming in his throat.

She gave a small smile and leaned forward to place her sweet lips, so soft and tender, against his forehead.

He fought the impulse to pull her closer

so he could press his lips against hers and explain without words all the emotions crowding his chest. Instead, he released her and allowed her to step away.

She handed him a cell phone. "I'll be right back with some food."

An unfamiliar ache filled him as she walked away. He was afraid when the time came for them to part for good, she would be taking his heart with her.

In an attempt to tamp down her worry, Abby paused outside the door to the bedroom where Jace was convalescing. She balanced the tray she held, carrying a bowl of soup and crackers. For hours, she'd held her breath, agonizing over Jace's injuries and fearing the cartel would return. But he was awake now. A good thing. Dr. Smithy promised to come up and check on Jace as soon as he finished with a patient downstairs.

She wasn't sure what Jace had been about to say earlier, but she was pretty sure it wasn't just words of gratitude. She couldn't believe how much she wanted to know if the word *love* would have been involved if he'd finished his sentence. But that was ridiculous. Her heart bumped with denial. Okay, maybe she'd grown more than fond of this man. But love?

No. She couldn't. She wouldn't. She straightened her spine and squared her shoulders with determination. They had to get out of here and back to their lives.

She had a job and friends and family waiting for her to return. And Daisy. Though as long as someone fed the cat, the feline would be okay.

Still, Abby wanted normal back. A life without danger or fear.

Yet what would normal be now?

She wasn't the same person who'd been attacked in the bank's parking lot one night. She'd changed, pushed herself beyond what she had imagined herself capable of. Would she be content with the life she'd once known?

Pushing open the door to the bedroom, she met Jace's unwavering gaze. She took in his beautiful battered and bruised face, and her heart pumped against her rib cage. So stubborn, yet so likable. A man of honor and integrity. The kind of man she'd dreamed of finding one day. The realization had her skin itching, but her hands were full, so she had to endure the suffering. "I hope you like chicken noodle."

"Yes. Mmm, smells good," Jace murmured.

Sitting on the edge of the bed, she balanced the tray across Jace's lap. "Do you want my help?"

He grinned. "I can manage to feed myself."

Telling herself she was staying close in case he needed her, she remained at his side. "Did you get ahold of your friend?"

"I did. He's on his way. He's also going to track down my father."

Had something happened to Marshal Armstrong? Her heart hurt to consider the possibility.

Jace crumbled a handful of crackers into the soup. "When I was in your apartment,

I noticed you had several travel books. Have you been to all those places?"

She bit her lip. Did she dare confess she was only an armchair traveler? Actually going anywhere filled her with anxiety. An almost comical notion after being on the run from a drug cartel for several days now. "I like to read about various places."

One corner of his mouth tipped up. "I take it that's a no."

She sighed. What harm would it do to tell him? "Until I got on the plane to go to Austin with you, the farthest I've traveled from home was to Disneyland. In California."

"Why?"

Purposely misunderstanding his question, she said, "We went there for my tenth birthday. And then again on Nancy's tenth birthday. It's the happiest place on earth, don't you know?"

His smile was patient, and he reached for her hand once again. As their fingers threaded around each other, she marveled at how natural and right the simple act of melding their hands together seemed, like something they'd done a million times. Her mind flashed to a scene in a popular older movie where they were interviewing elderly couples talking about their romance when they were young.

She nearly laughed aloud as the words *a drug cartel was trying to kill me when this cowboy came to my rescue, and I just knew, like you know about a good melon* ran through her mind.

"Why haven't you traveled to all the places you want to explore?"

Shrugging, she ignored the sting of embarrassment digging into her. "Oh, you know, the usual excuses. Time and money."

"Don't you get vacations?"

"I do." Stay vacations were more her speed than planning and executing a trip somewhere.

"Wouldn't your sister or your friend go with you?"

"Of course they would," she admitted. "It's just...several years ago I planned a trip. To Italy. My dream vacation. I was all set to go with a tour group. I'd made it onto the plane when I got the news that my father—" She swallowed as a swell of grief rose to clog her throat. "The man I called father had been diagnosed with cancer. I got off the plane as fast as I could. I was so afraid if I left, he would die before I got back. He died six months later."

"Understandable." After a beat, he said, "But you haven't traveled anywhere since his death?"

"Other than to the resort spot of Oilton, population three hundred?" She looked away from him, her gaze trained on the window. The orange-and-pink glow of the setting sun filtered through the lightweight curtain, making the room softer and rendering it easier to confess in the pretty light. "I've suffered with anxiety my whole life. I've only had two full-blown panic attacks. The rest of the time, it's just this low-level thing hanging out at the periphery of my consciousness. I've seen counselors and therapists. One doc-

tor said it was just part of my personality."
She shrugged and turned back to Jace.

There was no pity in his eyes, only understanding. "I've had my own battles
with anxiety over the years."

Surprise washed over her. "You? But
you seem so impervious to everything."

"Not impervious. I've learned to handle
it. Sort of." He gave a soft, wry chuckle.
"Whenever I'd get anxious as a child, I
would set out to find some daring adventure and legitimately get my heart
pumping. Jumping off a cliff into a river.
Riding my bicycle without hands down a
hill. Breaking in a new horse. Stealing the
neighbor's car. Hitchhiking from our family ranch to my father's office."

"Okay, I can imagine you doing those
things. Especially breaking in a new
horse." He was a cowboy, after all. "Even
the hitchhiking. But stealing your neighbor's car?" Though he had been prepared
to steal a muscle car a few days ago.

"It was an old pickup truck that sat
mostly unused. I was twelve and wanted

to drive to San Antonio to tell my dad he had to come home. We hadn't seen him in days, and I could tell my mom was worried. The neighbor didn't press charges when the town sheriff pulled me over. Though my dad wasn't nearly as understanding."

She would've liked to have known him as a preteen and teenager, all full of angst and apparent resentment toward his father's work. "And yet you became a marshal just like your dad."

He gave a rueful laugh. "What can I say? I wanted my father's attention. I wanted to make him proud." His lips twisted. "Still do, truth be told."

"I'm sure your dad's proud of you. I'm proud of you."

The tender expression in his eyes had her heart pumping. "You are a generous woman. As for my father, I doubt me failing to protect you will make him proud."

"You have not failed," she said, frustration beating against her temples. "I do not want to hear you say that ever again."

Jace dipped his chin. "Yes, ma'am."

"That's right. I'm the one in charge right now. You do as I say." She softened her words with a smile.

"You're not only a warrior, but a queen."

She laughed. "I doubt anybody would say I'm a warrior queen."

"You're my warrior queen."

Her heart thumped. She wasn't his anything, despite how much she wished with everything in her that she was.

Abruptly, she stood and tugged her hand from his. She grasped the tray with the nearly empty bowl of soup with shaky hands. The spoon rattled in the bowl. "You need to rest."

And she needed space from this much too handsome and appealing man who made her want to believe in a future with him.

TWELVE

Though Jace moved in and out of consciousness for the rest of the afternoon, he was aware of Abby coming and going. During his lucid moments, distress was his companion when he'd find the room empty. He hated that he wasn't recovered enough to protect her. He sent up a litany of prayers for protection over her and over the medical clinic. If the Garcia Cartel returned, would Miguel be able to keep them safe a second time?

Jace also prayed Brian would arrive soon with word of his father. Nightmares of what might've happened to his dad tormented his sleep. Tomas Garcia was counting on Gavin to find Carlos. Had his dad located the former cartel member?

Were they both still alive? Or were they in Garcia's custody?

The questions ran on a loop through his brain, making his rest uneasy. The next time he awoke, it was dark, and muted light from a streetlamp outside sneaked around the curtain's edge. He had a moment of disorientation, like the world was upside down. "Abby?"

There was a rustling off to his right. The bed dipped. He expected another wave of pain, but there was just a bit of throbbing. Hopefully, it was a good sign he was healing already.

A cool hand touched his forehead. "I'm here."

He yearned for more of her. He reached out until he connected with her, his fingers curling over her arm. Heavy material kept him from touching the warmth of her skin. "I can't see you."

She moved away, forcing him to release her. She snapped on the bedside lamp, and he flinched away from the sudden glow. "How long was I out this time?"

"Four hours at the most."

Lamplight glinted off her honey-blond hair. He liked her hair down and flowing around her shoulders. His fingers itched to run through the strands. A green cable-knit sweater hung on her slim shoulders.

"You're cold?"

"I did get a bit of a chill once the sun went down." She plucked at the sweater. "The doctor was kind enough to let me borrow it."

Jace vaguely recalled a gray-haired, bearded man checking his vitals. "What's my prognosis?"

Abby's soft smile made his stomach flip. So pretty, kind and brave.

"Good. Since your fever broke, Dr. Smithy says the antibiotics are doing their job. By the time your friend gets here, you should be well enough to move. Though you will still hurt from your injuries."

He'd deal with the pain. "Any word from my father?"

She shook her head, worry clear in her hazel eyes. She picked up the cell phone from the bedside table and glanced at it as if making sure she hadn't missed a call. "Nothing." She turned her bright gaze to him. "Do you want to call the San Antonio office?"

It was tempting to reach out, but he didn't want to risk the mole within the department obtaining information on where they were. He hoped the Laredo office hadn't been compromised. "No. We'll wait for Brian. He should be here soon."

The glare of headlights swung across the room, and the sound of an engine turning off sent Jace's heart rate into overdrive. Was the cartel back?

Abby moved to the window and pushed the curtain aside to peer out. Her forehead puckered. "A single man driving a dark sedan."

"What's he doing?"

"Just standing there next to the car."

Jace smiled. One of Brian's quirks. He never made a move without first letting all of his senses take stock of his surroundings. The extra care made him good at his job.

"He's wearing a Hawaiian-print shirt and shorts. Are those docksiders?"

"It's Brian." Only Brian would show up dressed like he was on a tropical vacation.

"He's walking toward the medical clinic now." Abby's voice held a note of worry.

From below, voices carried up the stairs.

Abby stood at the foot of the bed. "How will I know if it's your friend and not some ploy by the cartel?"

Jace appreciated her strategic mind. "Ask him who won the sharpshooter contest. If he says he did, he's lying. If he says I did, he's lying."

Abby made a face. "So neither of you did?"

"Nope," Jace happily told her. "The winner was a beauty named Seraphina Morales."

Abby stared at him for a long moment. "A girlfriend of yours?"

Jace barked out a soft laugh and then winced as it pulled at his ribs. "Hardly.

Sera went through the US Marshals basic training with Brian and me. She had a single-minded focus to best us all. At everything. She wasn't about to let—" he made air quotes with his fingers "—'pretty boys' derail her plans."

"Sounds like a smart lady. I already like her."

And Jace liked Abby. More than he should. But help was downstairs, and they needed to get out of here. He shooed her away with a flick of his hand. "Go bring that lughead up here."

"Lughead?"

"He likes to tinker with cars."

Abby gave a nod, stepped out of the room and closed the door softly behind her.

Jace used his elbows to force himself into a more vertical position. The muscles in his torso protested, but the pain was nothing like it had been before. By the time Abby returned with Brian in tow, Jace was sitting upright.

Brian filed in behind Abby. His friend

had the laid-back appearance of a beach bum with his sun-bleached hair and tanned skin.

"I take it he answered correctly?"

"He did." Abby sat in the chair.

"Thanks for coming, Bri," Jace said. "You have any trouble getting here?"

Brian lifted one sardonic eyebrow. "Dude, I was in the middle of an op when you called. It took a little finagling to get the powers that be to release me, and you know how LA traffic is. A crawl. Finally got on the plane and landed in Laredo to find several cartel dudes hanging out there."

"How do you know they were cartel?" Abby asked.

Brian shrugged. "Too many guys dressed in black in this heat. But they barely paid any attention to a guy in board shorts and an aloha shirt."

Jace breathed a sigh of relief. It would be easy to underestimate Brian. "It's good to see you, man. Were you able to reach my dad?"

Brian's normal jovial expression sobered. "Unfortunately, no. I even checked in with our friend Sera, who then discreetly asked around the San Antonio office. Nobody's seen or heard from him since early yesterday morning."

A clamp of dread squeezed Jace's chest. "Abby and I were the last to see him."

Fear chomped down hard on his insides. Would he be reunited with his dad? Regret for not telling his father how much he loved and respected him sliced a raw wound through Jace's heart. All the times Jace had rebelled against his dad's need for security stung. How often he'd railed against his father's devotion to the job over his family.

Jace had only ever wanted his dad's time and attention. He'd wanted to live in a world where fathers always had time to spend with their sons, and those sons never disappointed them. But now that Jace was hip deep in the weeds of the job, he understood his father's need to protect his wife and child. He understood and respected the sacrifice.

Though Jace wasn't married to Abby, he still had the same drive to keep her safe. He would sacrifice his life for her.

Abby moved to his bedside and took his hand. A shiver of longing ran a ragged course through him. He wanted to tug her closer and kiss her until all of his inner turmoil dissolved. However, reality kept him from moving. There was no world where he could claim more from Abby than he already had. His job was to protect her, and he needed to get her to safety.

"We have to have faith that he's okay." Her soft voice wrapped around him like a soothing blanket of warmth. "He's out searching for Carlos. He probably doesn't want anyone to be able to track him."

Jace gave her hand a squeeze. She always seemed to seek the brighter side of any situation. Her innate goodness was an alluring elixir to the fear and rage swirling inside him.

"There's a story there." Brian's gaze bounced from Jace to Abby and back.

"And I'd love to hear it on our way out of this place. Got a bad vibe when I pulled in."

"And we know how spot-on your vibes are," Jace said, forcing his legs over the side of the bed. Abby held on to his biceps, helping him to the edge of the mattress. He sat for moment, letting his equilibrium balance. Brian went to the window and pushed the curtain aside enough to check the street below.

"I'm sure I had shoes on when I arrived here," Jace said.

Abby gave a little start. "Of course. And a shirt." She hurried out of the room.

Surely his shirt was in tatters, if not ruined, after Marco's beating. Abby returned a few moments later with both his boots and a borrowed shirt. He allowed Abby to help him dress because it was hard to maneuver without causing a riot of slicing blades of pain cutting through him.

Or at least that was what he told himself as he breathed in her scent. She smelled so good. Gone were the hints of lavender and vanilla, replaced with a fresh, mouth-watering aroma that reminded him of the apple orchards on his family's ranch.

"There's activity down on the street."

Brian's grim tone yanked Jace's attention from Abby. "How many?"

"Hard to tell," he said. "I've stayed too long. I need to roll before they become suspicious and investigate."

"Leave," Jace said. "Circle back around to the rear of the building. We'll go out the back."

"You got it." Brian held up his cell phone. "Call me if the plan changes."

Jace turned to Abby. "Will the doc let us have his phone?"

She shrugged. "I can ask him."

"Good." To Brian, Jace said, "We'll see you shortly."

Brian acknowledged his words with a nod. "Do you have a weapon?"

"No."

Brian reached to his waistband and withdrew a Glock.

"You might need it."

Brian grinned. "You think I came packing only one gun?"

Jace held out his hand. Brian placed the piece on Jace's palm.

"Be safe," Jace said.

Brian saluted him and shut the door behind him.

With Abby's help, Jace got to his feet and held on to the four-poster bed as a wave of dizziness threatened to take him to his knees. When the world steadied, he tucked the weapon into the waistband of his jeans and pulled his shirt over the piece. "Help me to the window."

Abby moved closer, wrapping an arm gently around his waist. He put his arm around her shoulders, liking how well they fit together. At the window, he moved the curtain enough to give him a view of the street below. To the naked eye, the street appeared deserted.

A few moments later, Brian walked out carrying a small white paper bag and headed for his car. Two men wearing dark clothing materialized out of the shadows, waylaying him within the glow of the streetlight. Brian held up the bag and showed them the contents.

Jace's heart beat in his throat, and he prayed Brian's ability to talk his way out of dangerous situations would prevail. Would the thugs believe he'd only stopped for some medicine? At night?

After several moments of animated talking, Brian got into his vehicle and drove off. Jace released the breath he'd been holding. The two thugs remained in the street until the taillights of Brian's sedan disappeared down the highway. Then they shrank back into the shadows.

The cartel was staking out the town. It would be too much to hope the cartel wasn't surveilling the back of the building. They needed a new plan. He sent Brian a text telling him to hang tight and out of sight down the highway.

Tucking the cell phone the doctor had supplied them with into his front pants pocket, Jace said, "Help me downstairs."

"No," Abby replied with a frown. "Let

me go down to make sure it's safe. I will ask Dr. Smithy to close up. Nobody can see you. We told his patients I was his niece from New York."

Jace cupped her cheek. "Who'd have guessed you'd be so good at all this subterfuge."

She shrugged. "I watch a lot of crime shows, remember?"

He chuckled. "That you do." He sobered. "Still, knowing the cartel is out there, I don't like the idea of you going downstairs alone and unprotected."

She ducked out from under his arm, leaving him to lean against the wall while she went to the corner behind the door where a baseball bat had been propped up. He hadn't noticed it before, but then, he hadn't been looking for it. "After the cartel's visit this morning, Dr. Smithy gave me this."

"Do you know how to use it?" Would she be able to swing at someone? Or would her inherent compassion keep her from harming others?

She dipped her chin and arched an eyebrow. She lifted the bat over her shoulder and gave a mock swing. Every inch the warrior queen. "Not only did I play softball in grade school, but back at the Garcia compound, I clocked a guard with a table lamp."

Once again impressed with her, he tipped an imaginary hat. Her grin hit him like a line drive to the heart. She slipped out the door, and he pushed away from the wall, forcing his feet to work. Disliking the fact he'd sent her out with only a bat as her weapon, he made it across the room on his own and to the door. He couldn't in good conscience let her go down there unprotected. Now he just needed to make it down the stairs without falling and breaking his neck.

Abby kept the bat at her side as she descended the stairs. Dr. Smithy was in an exam room with a patient. The waiting area was empty. She breathed out a sigh of thanksgiving and hurried to the front door to flip the lock. Thankfully, Dr. Smithy had already closed the blinds on all the windows.

She hurried to the edge of the exam room and peeked inside. An elderly couple was talking with the doctor. All three heads swiveled toward her, and she grimaced inwardly.

"Sorry to interrupt, Uncle, but you have an urgent call," she said.

Dr. Smithy's gray eyebrows rose. He apologized to the couple and followed her out of the exam room into the kitchen.

"Your friend left with an antihistamine. Apparently, he has an allergy to sagebrush," Dr. Smithy said.

"The cartel has men watching the street," she whispered. "We need to get out of here."

Alarm flashed across Dr. Smithy's face, but then his brows lowered as he seemed to consider the situation. "The Navarros will give you and your man upstairs a ride."

"We can't ask that of them," she protested. She couldn't put more civilians in danger.

"They will be glad to help," the doctor assured her. "Not everyone around here is loyal to the Garcias."

"But how do we leave without the men out front catching us?"

"We'll come up with a plan."

"Can we keep the cell phone?"

"Of course. I'll use the landline until I can get a replacement." The doctor turned and headed back to the exam room, and Abby had no choice but to follow.

"Beth and Neil, this is my niece visiting from New York. She and her beau need to get out of town. They've had a bit of *trouble*." The way he emphasized *trouble* left no doubt that his words meant their trouble had been with the Garcia Cartel.

Beth's forehead creased with obvious concern. She was a stout woman with dark hair and kind eyes. "How can we help?"

The doctor took her hand. "Bless you."

A noise from the stairs reached them, prickling Abby's skin. Jace. She ducked out of the room and found Jace awkwardly descending the stairs.

"What are you doing?"

"Are you okay?" he asked. Sweat dripped off his brow.

"I'm fine," she ground out and helped him the rest of the way. "You are so stubborn. That was risky of you to try on your own."

Clearly unrepentant, he said, "Does the doc have a car?"

"We're getting a ride," she told him.

Dr. Smithy ushered Jace and Abby into the exam room and made introductions to Beth and Neil.

"We've discussed the options and came up with a plan. You two will leave here pretending to be the Navarros." He handed Abby a dark-colored beanie. "You need to hide your hair."

Heart hammering, Abby slipped the beanie on; Beth helped to tuck her hair beneath the edges. A ball of nerves tangled in Abby's stomach.

Neil handed Jace the keys to his truck.

"We're parked in the back lot. The red truck."

Though Neil was tall, Jace had to hunch his shoulders to match his height. "We'll somehow get the truck back to you."

"Losing the truck will be a small sacrifice," Neil said. "You two stay safe."

Handing Abby a bag, Dr. Smithy said, "Some protein bars. You'll need to keep up your strength."

Beth pulled Abby into a hug. "We'll pray for you."

How much had the doctor told the older couple? Abby clung to her for a moment, suddenly missing her own mother. Though angry and hurt as Abby had been when she'd learned that her mother had kept an important detail of Abby's life a secret, Abby loved her mother and prayed she and Nancy were safe. The yearning to be reunited with her family had Abby's chest aching.

With the bag in hand, Abby and Jace hurried out of the medical clinic's back door. The red truck was the only vehicle in the lot. Jace slid into the driver's seat with a soft hiss of pain that arrowed straight through Abby. She hesitated a moment. Should she drive? But would that signal to the cartel members that something wasn't right?

With quick steps, she went around to the passenger door. Movement in the shadows near the garbage dumpster stalled her breath. She jumped inside, shut the door and locked it, but she didn't breathe any easier. The old truck wouldn't stop bullets.

After using the doc's phone to text Brian they were on their way, Jace fired up the truck, threw it into gear and pressed on the gas. Abby turned her face away from the side window and hunkered down, afraid the streetlight might reveal that she wasn't Beth Navarro.

They drove in silence down the main street away from the clinic, every second ticking by with excruciating tension.

"So far, so good," Jace said as they left the town behind.

She had no idea where they were headed. "Do we know where to meet Brian?"

"His text said somewhere along this road."

A short time later, the headlights of the old truck brought into view Brian's dark sedan sitting on the side of the road. Jace killed the lights and pulled the truck over. Abby jumped out and ran around the front of the truck as Jace climbed out. She slid an arm around his waist. He tensed but allowed her to steady him.

Brian hopped out of the sedan to open the back passenger door.

Headlights appeared on the road coming from the town.

"Get in. Hurry!"

Brian's shout jarred through Abby, and she shoved Jace into the back seat, dived in next to him and slammed the door. Brian revved up the car, and they took off in a spray of gravel.

THIRTEEN

Abby hung on to Jace for dear life as Brian's sedan roared down the highway at a breakneck speed without headlights. A risky endeavor. Did they have deer in Texas?

The bright headlights of the vehicle behind them sent a shiver of alarm and dread slithering through her. Any second now, the cartel could start shooting at them or run them off the road and then kill them all.

"Hang on," Brian shouted and cranked the wheel. The sedan skidded as they turned off the main road, the tires squealing on the pavement until they found purchase on gravel. The car incrementally slowed as if Brian had taken his foot off the gas.

Abby peered out the back window as two big black SUVs sped past the dirt-and-gravel road they'd turned onto.

The sedan kept bumping along until it finally came to a stop and Brian put it in Park. "You two okay?"

The ambient glow of the moon provided enough light for Abby to maneuver herself to a sitting position. Jace was breathing hard. She could only imagine what this little escapade had cost him in pain. She helped him right himself on the seat.

"We're good, buddy." Jace's voice was strained.

Brian nodded. "We'll give it a few minutes. Then we'll head out again."

Jace powered off the doctor's cell phone, then removed the SIM card and broke it in two. He tossed the phone and card pieces out the window.

As they waited in the dark surrounded by the desert landscape, Abby's heart rate began to decelerate. "Will the cartel double back?"

Jace put his arm around her shoulders. "Don't worry—we'll get out of this."

She doubted he was going to take his own advice about not worrying.

After a few minutes, Brian popped the car into Drive, made a three-point turn and headed them back toward the highway leading out of Oilton.

"You both should stay down," Brian advised. "Just in case."

Jace hissed as he scooted back down to where his head was below the seat. Abby followed suit. He tugged her closer, his arm encircling her and his fingers firm against her biceps. She rested her head against the space between his chest and his shoulder.

An hour later, they were in the center of Laredo, the bright lights of the city shining through the sedan's windows.

"We have a few choices," Brian said at a stoplight. "We can find a place to lie low for the night and head out again in the morning. We can start driving toward San Antonio now and get there sometime in the wee hours of the morning, but we'll be exposed on the highway. We could take an indirect route, which would eat up more time. Or we can head to the airport and take the first flight out."

"None of those options sound particularly safe." Abby just wanted to go home and put this all behind her. She feared that confronting the cartel would end in tragedy.

"We do have to make a decision," Jace said, his voice soft against her hair.

The rumble of his voice inside his chest reverberated against her cheek. It was too dark to discern his expression, but she could sense his expectation. He was letting her make the call. Her heart bumped against her ribs. For a man who liked to be in control, this was an unexpected move. Affection and gratitude twined through her like a ribbon, tying her up in knots. His certainty of her made her braver.

"How do we fly without ID?" she asked.

Brian answered, "I can handle that."

He sounded so confident, she believed him. "It might be safest to go to the airport, where there are more people and security," she finally said, bracing for the men to explain why she should have chosen a different option.

Jace gave her a squeeze. "You heard the lady, Bri."

"The airport it is."

Jace wasn't surprised when Brian brought the sedan to a halt at the baggage claim area. No doubt the cartel would be surveilling the arrival deck. If they had a man monitoring this level, the guy would stand out like a sore thumb. People exiting the terminal had bags in tow.

Ignoring the pain reverberating through his body, Jace followed Abby out of the vehicle and headed toward the rotating doors leading into the Laredo baggage claim.

"Hey, you can't leave your car there," a

female airport security officer called as she strode toward them.

"I've got this," Brian said. "You get inside."

Jace hurried Abby inside the terminal. No doubt Brian would charm the cop and find a way to show her his badge without alerting anyone who might be observing.

Hustling Abby to the elevator rather than the escalator, Jace kept her tucked close. The escalator was too open, and they'd be too vulnerable. They took the elevator to the upper level.

The doors opened, and he held up a hand, stalling her a moment so he could peek out of the elevator. Scanning the passengers, he noticed two men loitering near the security gate. Both were dressed in casual clothing that didn't make them stand out, but there was something in the way they scrutinized those passing by. Were they searching for him and Abby?

A family of tourists, a mother, father and two teens, approached.

Jace grabbed Abby's hand. "Keep your head down. We've got company."

He tugged her out of the elevator, and they fell into step alongside the family, aware of the curious glances of the parents. The teens were oblivious, each with headphones jammed in their ears.

Keeping his shoulders hunched so that he didn't tower over their cover, Jace kept Abby moving at a slow pace until the family peeled off and headed for one of the popular airlines.

Jace headed to the last ticket counter for a smaller commercial airline. Keeping Abby shielded by his body, he texted Brian the name of the airline.

They had to wait for Brian so he could secure their tickets, since neither Jace nor Abby had any money or ID. Brian showed his US Marshals badge when he handed over his credit card and explained he was escorting witnesses to San Antonio.

The woman behind the counter hesitated.

Brian handed her a card. "Call that number."

Jace held his breath as they waited while the woman made the call verifying Brian's credentials.

After ending the call, the wide-eyed ticket agent handed three tickets to Brian.

They moved away from the ticket counter. "Who did she call?" Jace asked.

"Sera," Brian replied with a grin. "I texted her to let her know to expect the call."

"How do we get past the two thugs standing at the security entrance?" Abby asked.

"Already taken care of." Brian smirked. "The cop was more than happy to send officers to question them at the gate."

Jace clapped him on the back. "Thanks, man."

They made it to the gate without mishap, and an hour and twenty minutes later, they boarded a small jet to San Antonio. After landing, they debarked and headed out of the terminal. Despite the protein bars the doctor had given them, Jace's energy had dwindled.

"Our ride is here." Brian waved, and a nondescript brown sedan pulled to the curb. He opened the back passenger door.

Abby raised her eyebrows but slid into the sedan. Jace joined her in the back as Brian sat in the front passenger seat.

Seraphina Morales sat behind the steering wheel with her straight dark hair held back by a clip. Heavily tinted sunglasses covered her eyes. "Hello. Glad you're all in one piece."

"We're glad to see you," Jace said. "Sera, this is Abby. Abby, this is Sera."

Abby sat forward. "I understand you can outshoot these two."

Sera grinned and stepped on the gas, merging the sedan into the flow of traffic. "I'm surprised they mentioned it. Nice to meet you, Abby. Where are we headed?"

"To my family's ranch," Jace said. It was the safest place. At Abby's quizzical expression, he grinned, despite the bundle of nerves tangling in his gut and the aches in his body. "I'm going to make good on my promise. You're going to meet my mother."

The drive from the San Antonio airport was filled with conversation, mostly between Brian and Sera, much to Abby's amusement. The two wove hilarious tales of their exploits during their academy days. Jace would occasionally join in, but he remained vigilant. Tension radiated off him and had Abby's nerves jangling. Surely she was safe with three armed US marshals?

After he made a quick call using Sera's cell to let his mother know they were coming, Jace lapsed into silence.

They left the city limits, driving on a stretch of highway taking them past long areas of land with cattle or horses grazing. The scenery was stunning. Under other circumstances, she'd be more appreciative, but she couldn't shake the sense of dread cramping her chest.

Sera turned off the main road and drove beneath a large metal archway reading Camp Strong.

"Camp Strong?"

"After I left home, being alone was too much for Mom. She started a horse camp for at-risk youth."

Morning sunlight required Abby to shield her eyes. Lush pastureland with grazing horses and an inviting orchard took Abby's breath away. There were two arenas and little cabins forming a half circle around a centerpiece firepit. The main house was a stunning two-story Craftsman with a wraparound porch. As they came to a halt at the front steps of the house, a woman came out the front door.

Mrs. Armstrong was a surprise. Abby wasn't sure what she'd expected. The petite woman with a long red braid hanging over her shoulder wore jeans, cowboy boots, a Western-style plaid shirt and a pink cowboy hat. The whole effect reminded Abby of a character from a popular animated kids' movie. Abby would guess young people would find Jace's mother approachable and endearing. Even from this distance, a tug on Abby's heart had her longing to know this woman.

Jace slowly climbed out of the vehicle and moved gingerly forward to engulf his mother in a hug. His mother put a hand to his face, no doubt asking about his injuries. Clearly, he got his height from his father.

Abby followed Sera and Brian to where Jace and his mother stood as the two turned toward them.

Keeping his arm around his mom's shoulders, Jace said, "Mom, this is Abby Frost. Abby, my mother, Victoria." He gave a chin nod toward the other two people. "Of course, you know Brian and Sera."

"Yes, of course. Bri and Sera." Victoria's smile grew even wider as she met Abby's gaze. "Hello. I'm so glad y'all are here."

Sera stepped forward to hug Victoria. "It's been a long time."

"That it has," Victoria said. "You know you're welcome to come ride anytime."

"I appreciate the offer." Sera moved aside so Brian could also hug Victoria.

"How's life in California?"

Brian tucked his hands in his board shorts pockets. "Lots of sunshine."

Victoria's gaze landed on Abby again. There was a speculative gleam in her bright green eyes. She held out a hand, urging Abby to move forward.

"It's nice to meet you. Gavin mentioned you're having a rough time," Victoria said, her warm hand closing over Abby's.

Surprise at learning Marshal Armstrong had spoken to his wife about her washed over Abby, and she wasn't sure how to respond.

Thankfully, Victoria didn't miss a beat. Her gaze encompassed Jace, Brian and Sera. "Come inside for breakfast. I've got fixings for an omelet bar." She tucked Abby's hand into the crook of her arm and led her inside.

The interior of the house was just as

charming as the outside. Gleaming cherrywood floors and Western-style furniture appeared comfy but upscale. The kitchen was impressive. A large island with a quartz countertop in white with a silver vein added a touch of whimsy in the middle of the room with a row of bar stools. A stainless-steel dishwasher and a double farm-style sink sat beneath a large window framed by pretty silver-and-white curtains. The cabinets were painted in a soft dove gray. The whole effect was something from one of the interior designer magazines her sister, Nancy, loved to peruse.

"Your home is lovely," Abby said, taking a seat on a counter stool. Jace carefully took the stool to her right, while Brian and Sera planted themselves on the two remaining seats.

Victoria set empty plates in front of them and waved a hand toward a buffet bar with chafing dishes. "Help yourselves."

Brian didn't waste a moment. He picked up his plate and headed for the food.

Sera chuckled. "The man has always had a bottomless pit."

Jace didn't move, and Abby remained in place, waiting for his lead.

"Have you heard from Dad?"

Concern flashed across Victoria's pretty face. "No." She shot a glance at Abby and then looked back at Jace. "I'm really worried. This is unusual. He normally calls twice a day, but there's been nothing for the past twenty-four hours."

Abby's chest tightened. Beside her, Jace's fists clenched. "We haven't been able to get ahold of him, either." He started to stand but then stopped. "What do you mean he calls twice a day?"

His mother gave him a quizzical stare. "Your dad and I made a pact years ago. No matter what he's doing or where he is, he checks in with me once in the morning and once in the evening."

Abby thought their pact a sweet idea.

"I didn't know."

Jace's strange tone had Abby searching his face for the cause.

Victoria came around the island and put a hand on his arm. "Why else would your father and I have those burner phones?"

"I thought they were for emergencies only."

"For you they were for emergencies only. Your father didn't want to burden you with the responsibility of waiting for a phone call from him."

Jace's jaw clenched. Abby sensed there was turmoil going on in him that had nothing to do with the cartel and everything to do with being kept in the dark. It was a sentiment she understood. She'd been kept in the dark about her parentage all her life. The shock of learning the truth still had the power to squeeze her heart.

"It would've been nice to know." He slid off the stool with a hiss but shook off mother's attempt to steady him and headed to the buffet table.

His mother stared after him, a frown marring her brow. She turned to Abby. "Are you not hungry, dear?"

Abby scrambled off the counter stool and grabbed her plate. "I am, thank you."

Victoria put on coffee while Sera and Brian kept up an animated conversation about sports. Abby didn't pay attention to them; instead her focus was on Jace. He'd turned pensive and pushed his food around his plate.

She wished she were free to ask him what was wrong. Free to offer him comfort. Free to tell him how much she was coming to care for him. But she wasn't for so many reasons. Their lives had different trajectories. Hers would resume back in Washington, and he would remain in Texas. He'd told her he wasn't interested in a future that included marriage, and she wouldn't settle for anything less. He was a risk-taking protector who put his life on the line for others, while she was a boring banker, content to read about adventures rather than experience them.

Though, she could hardly say the past week hadn't been an adventure.

Instead of speaking or reaching for Jace,

she drank her coffee and tried to pretend the world was right side up, when deep inside it felt upside down.

Victoria set her own mug down and pinned Jace with worry furrowing her brow. "Do you have any idea where your father could be?"

Jace shook his head. "He's searching for a witness. But I don't know where his search has taken him."

"You have to find him," his mother insisted. "Abby will be safe here with me."

A protest rose on Abby's lips, but she held her words back. She didn't want Jace to leave her side. He was in no shape to go off doing anything. He wasn't fully recovered from the beating he'd taken. But what he did or didn't do wasn't her call.

"We'll search for Gavin," Brian offered, his gaze going to Sera, who nodded her agreement.

"We'll all go," Jace stated.

Brian shook his head. "You need to stay here and get a little more R & R. You look like ten miles of bad road, buddy."

Abby wanted to hug Brian for his perceptiveness.

Jace stared at his friend for a moment before slanting a glance in her direction. She held his gaze, silently imploring him not to insist on going to find his father.

He gave a sharp nod. "That would be best. Abby and I should lie low. We don't know who in my father's office is feeding intel to the drug cartel."

His mother made a face.

"Mom? You have a thought?"

His mother waved a hand as if dismissing whatever had popped into her mind. "Don't mind me."

Abby's heart sped up. "There is a thing called women's intuition. If someone comes to mind, it could be worth checking out."

Victoria held her gaze, her smile full of approval. "I like you, Abby." Victoria turned her focus on Jace. "I don't have anything concrete. But— It's silly even saying anything."

"Please, Mom," Jace prompted.

Victoria sighed. "I've always had a notion Regina wanted your father to herself."

The name rang a bell. The woman who'd answered the phone the first time Abby had called the San Antonio marshals service.

"But she's worked with Dad for years and is married with kids," Jace said, his brow furrowed. "Why would she betray his trust now?"

"Maybe because your father's getting ready to retire and is going to leave her behind." Victoria made another face. "Goodness, I sound like a jealous shrew."

"No, you don't," Abby said. "You sound like a woman who loves her husband and is worried about him."

Jace rubbed a hand over his jaw. "It's worth checking into." He turned to Brian and Sera. "Can you audit Regina's financial records? The cartel could be paying her for information."

Sera nodded. "Consider it done. In fact, I'll dig into everyone in the office."

"We'll call you if we come up with anything," Brian said. To Victoria, he added, "We'll find Gavin. And we'll find the mole. You have my word on it."

Brian and Sera said goodbye and headed out the door. A few moments later, the sound of tires on the gravel drive announced their departure.

"Abby, let me show you to a room," Victoria said. She moved past Jace, patting him gently on the shoulder. "You need to heal, not to mention a shower and a shave."

Abby's lips twitched. Only a mother could get away with saying that to a grown man.

Jace rolled his eyes after his mother. Then he grinned at Abby. "She's not wrong."

Abby couldn't stop from grinning back at him. "No, she's not."

"Hey, now." He feigned being wounded

by putting a hand over his heart. "You don't have to agree with me."

"We both have a bit of the stink on us," she said in her best imitation drawl.

His laugh warmed her heart as she followed Victoria upstairs.

FOURTEEN

The late afternoon sun heated Abby's face, but it was anticipation and trepidation that had her overheating as she eyed the big roan horse Jace had saddled for her, despite his injuries. The stubborn man refused to let the trauma of the past few days keep him from playing the perfect host. After they had both showered and dressed in fresh clothes, Jace had taken her on a nice slow walking tour of the ranch, explaining how his mother's camp operated.

Victoria was between sessions, so there were currently no campers in residence, but there was a lot of work to be done. Abby couldn't help the shot of envy for his mother. She was doing something so beneficial for so many others. Abby's life as a banker didn't really seem all that rewarding in retrospect.

Oh sure, she'd received awards and accolades for her service to the bank, so her job satisfied whatever need she might have to succeed, but was it enough?

While she and Lisa and Nancy volunteered through their church doing a toy drive every year for Christmas, it occurred to Abby living a life of service meant more than just putting yourself out there once a year. When she returned home, she'd seek more opportunities to give of her time. Nothing like a brush with death to make a woman reevaluate her life.

Jace looked every inch the cowboy in denim, a distressed-washed long-sleeve Henley shirt and a brown cowboy hat. The bruises on his face didn't detract from his handsomeness nor from his persuasive powers. He had talked her into learning how to ride after he'd discovered she'd never been on a horse.

Thankfully, Victoria had found appropriate clothing to fit Abby. The well-worn boots fit snugly but were not overly tight. A pair of jeans with a rip in the thigh molded to her like they were tailor-made for her. One of Jace's chambray shirts, tied at the waist and with the sleeves rolled up, completed the outfit. Jace had even wrangled up a black cowboy hat with flowers glued to the front for her, undoubtedly left by one of the kids. Both thrilled and dismayed, she couldn't believe she'd let him talk her into trying to ride a horse.

After checking the saddle and dropping down the stirrup, Jace motioned to the wooden steps he'd called a mounting block next to Abby. "Up you go."

"I'm not ready for this. It was an exciting idea to learn to ride—in theory. But..." She eyed the beast again. Her hooves pawed at the ground. Jace held the reins in one hand, stroking the horse's head with the other, no doubt to keep the mare calm. Abby wished Jace would put his arm around her to keep her calm. "What if I fall off?"

"You'll only fall off if you don't hang on."

She scrunched up her nose. "What if she bucks me off?"

"She will not buck you off." Jace moved closer and cupped Abby's cheek. His thumb slid along her bottom lip, and her mouth went dry. "Do you trust me?" he asked softly.

Bemused, she nodded. She'd come to trust this man with her life. He wouldn't let anything happen to her. Her heart thumped as he dipped his head.

He was going to kiss her. Did she want him to? Certainty washed over her like the warm Texas breeze she was growing accustomed to. Yes. Yes, she did. She went on tiptoe, her breath trapped in her chest as anticipation revved through her veins.

The horse nickered.

Jace stilled, meeting her gaze. He blinked, then straightened.

Disappointment rushed through her,

heating her cheeks. She should be thankful one of them had come to their senses. Apparently, her interpretation of his feelings for her was off-kilter. It was just as well. She had no business letting the attraction between them become something tangible. Something that could morph into more than just affection and care.

She turned to face the saddled horse, forcing him to remove his hand from her face. He backed away, giving her room.

With shaky hands, she stepped up on the mounting block and gripped the sides of the saddle like he'd shown her.

He held out the reins. "Take these in your left hand and put your left foot in the stirrup."

Gripping the reins as well as the horn on the Western saddle, she took a deep breath and stuck her foot into the stirrup.

"Now pull yourself up, swing your leg over, sit down and place your right foot in the stirrup on the other side."

Once both of her feet were settled into

the stirrups, she shifted on the saddle. "Not exactly a cushy seat."

He laughed. "You need to relax. You're sitting so upright, so of course the saddle's going to be uncomfortable."

She rolled her eyes and her shoulders, letting out a breath and trying to relax into the seat. It did help.

Jace clucked his tongue, and the horse moved forward. She gave a little yelp of surprise. "Warn me next time."

"What fun would that be?"

She eyed his grin. His charm blunted her momentary irritation. She held on to the pommel as Jace sedately walked the horse around the arena.

A sense of pride engulfed her. She was actually sitting on a horse while it was moving. She could now say she'd ridden a horse. If one could call this riding. But she'd take the win.

The sound of tires kicking up gravel drew their attention as a big black SUV roared down the drive, creating a wake of dust.

Was it the cartel? Fear slid along her limbs, making her shake. The horse seemed to sense her agitation and began to prance sideways. "Jace?"

Jace made soothing sounds, but Abby wasn't sure if they were for her or the horse. "It's only Brian. Nothing for us to be scared about."

Abby sent up a prayer, hoping his words were true. Jace turned to her. "Remember how to dismount?"

She eyed the distance to the ground and swallowed. "Can she just take me to the mounting block so I can step off?"

"Nope." He talked her through how to dismount, his hands coming to rest on her waist as she swung her right leg over the horse's rear end and then leaned over the saddle to take her left foot out of the stirrup. His warm hands guided her gently to the ground.

When her feet were on solid earth, she expected him to let go and step back so she could turn to face him. Instead, he placed a soft kiss on the back of her head.

"You did great."

His voice cocooned her like a comfortable sweater. The yearning to turn and wrap her arms around him was strong, but then he did slip his hands from her waist and step away. He took the reins from her and dropped them to the ground. She turned and gave him a quizzical look.

"Ground-tying trained. She won't move until I come back to lead her to her stall," Jace explained and strode to where Brian stood waiting, having exited the now parked SUV.

Abby had to take two steps to every one of Jace's to keep up.

No longer dressed as a surfer from California, Brian now wore cowboy boots, jeans, a buttoned-down shirt and a tan cowboy hat. He appeared every inch the Texan. He hustled forward, meeting them halfway.

"I've got a message from your dad," Brian said by way of greeting.

Abby's breath caught in her throat.

"He's safe?" Victoria came up behind

them, her question pulling their gazes to her. Abby wasn't sure if Victoria was breathing hard because she'd hurried from the house or from anticipation of news about her husband.

"He is," Brian said. "But he needs Jace and Abby to come to Houston, pronto."

"Then what are you waiting for?" Victoria chastised. "Get a move on, people. Bring your father home, Jace."

The drive to Houston was fraught with tension. Sitting in the front passenger seat while Brian drove, Jace kept an eye on the side mirror for any sort of tail. His father had summoned them to Houston, and Jace could only guess that meant he'd found Carlos.

Abby sat silently in the back passenger seat, dressed adorably in the Western clothes his mother had supplied for her. The memory of that moment in the corral, her face turned up to his, her lips parting in preparation for a kiss, had Jace's pulse skipping along his limbs like a kid chasing a butterfly.

He'd wanted to kiss her so badly, but then his father's voice had echoed through his mind, reminding him to be careful of her heart. Kissing her wouldn't have been smart.

He'd been helpless to stop himself from inhaling the scent of her as he'd helped her dismount, nor had he been able to keep from placing his lips against her hair. He'd had to curb the temptation to turn her in his arms and claim her mouth. Nothing good would come from allowing any more of an attachment to form between them.

Thankfully, they reached the city without incident. Three times, they circled the block of the restaurant where his father wanted to meet before Brian finally parked behind the building. Instead of going around to the front entrance, they went through the kitchen.

Brian showed his badge, paving the way for Jace to hustle Abby past all the curious and speculative stares of the staff and into the dining room.

Jace's gaze swept the booths and tables until he located his father in the corner to his far right. He breathed a sigh of relief. His dad was unharmed, though he needed a shave and there were dark circles beneath his eyes. Meeting his father's gaze, Jace gave a nod. Gavin slipped out of the booth and stood. Placing a hand at Abby's lower back, Jace moved her forward.

Awareness of the other man sitting in the shadows of the booth prompted Jace to slow.

Carlos Reyes.

His dark hair was streaked with gray, his shoulders hunched, and his hazel eyes were very similar to Abby's.

Abby stopped when her gaze landed on her biological father, forcing Jace to come to a halt.

"It's good to see you in one piece, son," Gavin said and pulled him in for a quick hug. "You look awful."

"Thanks, Dad," Jace replied, trying not to wince at the contact. "Call Mom."

"Already did."

Gavin released Jace and turned his attention to Abby. "Miss Frost, I'd like to introduce you to Carlos Reyes."

The older gentleman slid out of the booth. He was taller than he had appeared while seated, especially when he straightened his spine and squared his shoulders to meet his daughter.

"You look just like your mother." The soft voice sounded thick with emotion, as if it was clogging his throat.

"Thank you," Abby said, her tone polite.

Carlos swept a hand toward the booth. "Please sit."

Abby slipped into the booth, and Jace followed her. Carlos also slid into the booth from the other direction so that he and Abby were sitting across from each other. Gavin took a seat next to Carlos. Brian stood sentry, leaning casually against the booth's backrest at Jace's shoulder, effectively blocking the restaurant occupants' view of Abby.

Carlos ran a hand over his bristled jaw. "How is your mother?"

"She was good," Abby said, her voice now brittle. "But then I learned about you. I don't know how she is at the moment. Safe, I hope."

"This was what I was trying to avoid," Carlos said. His shoulders slumped. "I loved your mother very much. She deserved better. I hope she found happiness."

Abby seemed to hesitate. Then she reached across the table, her palm up in invitation.

Surprise washed over Carlos's face, and he slipped his hand into hers.

Abby's slender fingers curled around her father's. "She has had a good life," Abby said. She sounded determined to conquer whatever pain not knowing her real father had inflicted on her. "I know you did what you thought was best at the time."

Jace marveled at this woman's capacity to extend grace and compassion. She could have been very angry at this man who had caused such chaos in her life.

"What now?" Jace asked his father.

Gavin turned to stare at Carlos. "Tell them."

"I'm tired of running," Carlos stated. He sat up straighter. "I'm ready to do what I should've done thirty years ago."

His gaze snapping back to his father, Jace asked, "What about the mole in the department?"

"I have some ideas about the person's identity," Gavin said.

"So do I," Jace remarked. Did they suspect the same person? Would his father believe Regina, his longtime assistant, could be culpable?

"I have a plan," his father said.

Three days later, Abby put on the dress suit and heels she'd ordered off the internet using Victoria Armstrong's account. The A-line dress with matching jacket in a pretty aubergine color complemented her skin tone. She'd gathered a portion of her hair, clipped it at the crown of her head and left the rest down around her shoulders. Victoria had offered her an unopened lip gloss. For the first time in days, Abby could almost pretend everything was normal. It wasn't, of course. Nothing about this situation could be categorized as typical. Certainly not the trepidation sliding along her nerves.

They would head to San Antonio's courthouse soon, where Carlos Reyes would give testimony in front of a grand jury regarding the murder he'd witnessed thirty years ago. They were expecting an indictment to be handed down on Marco Garcia.

Abby's nerves fluttered, making the hearty breakfast Victoria had insisted she eat riot in her stomach. Jace and Abby would also testify before the same grand jury about being kidnapped by Tomas Garcia as well as Jace's assault by Marco.

This ordeal would be over soon, and she'd be able to resume her life.

For the past three days, Abby had spent time with her biological father at the Armstrong ranch. He'd shared with her about his life after fleeing the marshals service. He'd worked transient jobs, shuffling from one state to the next, trying to stay a step ahead of Garcia's hunt for him. Abby could only imagine how exhausting it had been. She also thought about the life she might have had if he'd not run. Nancy never would've been born. Abby couldn't imagine the world without her sister in it.

Abby had to trust things had worked out the way they were meant to. God, in His infinite wisdom, had put it upon Carlos to sacrifice the woman he loved for her safety.

Abby smoothed a hand down the front of her dress. All the years Dan Frost had spent loving her and providing for her even though she wasn't his child by blood made her miss him. She wished she'd had one last chance to tell him how grateful she was to have had him in her life. She let go of any resentment for the way he'd pushed her to succeed.

There was a soft knock at the bedroom door. "Come in."

The door opened, and Victoria Armstrong walked in, bringing with her a vitality and energy her son had clearly inherited from her. She wore jeans, a bright fuchsia shirt with little tassels on the pockets, well-worn cowboy boots and a pink cowboy hat. Her red hair was in a low ponytail. The whole effect made her appear much younger than her midsixties. Abby could only hope she would be as energetic and spry as this woman in thirty years.

Victoria returned her grin. "I have campers coming today." She gestured to her outfit. "This sends a message to the young girls they can trust me and I don't take myself too seriously."

"Cowboy casual works for you." Abby's admiration for Jace's mother grew.

"The men are ready for you downstairs," Victoria said. She held out her hands.

Abby hesitated. She would rather stay here than face the courthouse.

"You've got this," Victoria said. "You

have to trust Jace and Gavin and the others won't let anything happen to you or your father."

Her father. He was still a stranger to her, but she understood what Victoria was saying. Abby grasped Victoria's hands. "I do trust them."

"And Jace?" Victoria cocked her head. "You and my son are becoming very close."

Heat infused Abby's cheeks. "He's doing his job."

"I know my son." Victoria gave Abby's hand a squeeze. "He wouldn't have broken protocol by bringing you here if he didn't care for you. He could've easily taken you straight to the marshals' headquarters in downtown San Antonio, and they could've spirited you away to some unknown location across the country. Jace wanted to be by your side."

Unsure of what to say to Victoria's assessment of the situation, Abby stayed silent. Was it true? Did Jace's feelings for her go beyond duty?

The way he'd gazed at her the other day in the corral popped into her mind. There'd been emotions in his eyes she hadn't had time to comprehend. She'd been too thrilled by the prospect of a kiss, but now she reflected on what his expression meant. Could he care for her the way she was coming to care for him?

And care she did. More than care, if she were being honest with herself. But now was not the time to contemplate all the emotions crowding her chest, making her heart rate ramp up and increasing her nervousness.

"I know my son is hesitant to get involved with anyone long-term. Growing up the son of a marshal was hard. I'm not going to lie," Victoria stated in a matter-of-fact tone. "There are times I am lonely. There are times when I fear something will happen to Gavin, but that's the nature of the job."

Victoria shrugged. "I understood the risks going in. Gavin and I never wanted to burden Jace with the dangerous aspects, but by protecting him, we made him more anxious."

Her mouth quirked. "I had hoped Jace would grow up and become a doctor or rancher, anything other than a lawman, but it must be handed down through the genes. Gavin's father was also a lawman. He passed long before I met Gavin."

Absorbing Victoria's words, Abby ached for young Jace. "You could be right about it being in the genes," Abby stated softly. "Jace admires Gavin so very much. He was very worried when he disappeared."

"As was I. But my faith is strong." Victoria turned toward the door, releasing one of Abby's hands and tucking the other one through her arm. They walked out of the bedroom and down the hall.

In a low voice, Victoria said, "If you care for my son, you'll figure out a way to be together. Don't let his fear keep you apart."

Abby slanted her a surprised glance and pressed her lips together. Victoria's words reverberated through Abby's mind, but she had no chance to process before they entered the living room, where Jace, his father, Carlos and Brian stood waiting. All four men were dressed in suits.

Abby couldn't take her eyes off Jace. He'd shaved his strong jaw, and his face still bore bruises, thanks to the beating he'd taken, but the marks were fading. His hair had been tamed back, and a navy suit hugged his wide shoulders and narrowed down to his trim waist. The navy slacks outlined his powerful legs. The tips of a pair of cowboy boots sticking out from beneath the hem of his trousers had her grinning.

When she met his gaze, he grinned back. He shrugged. "You can take the cowboy out of the pasture, but you can't take the cowboy out of the man."

Brian made a face. "Dude, that doesn't make sense." He moved to the front door. "We best hurry if we want this plan to work. Sera has everything all set."

Though they were preparing for the Garcia Cartel to show up at the hearing, she wasn't exactly sure what the marshals' plans included. As she folded her fingers around Jace's, she could only pray nothing went wrong, because she had a suspicion her biggest adventure was yet to come.

FIFTEEN

Waiting to be called before the grand jury ratcheted up Jace's tension. The heels of his cowboy boots clicked on the marble floor as he paced the hallway of the courthouse. With each pass, he stole glances at Abby. She sat on a wooden bench placed along the wall outside the grand jury's chamber. She looked so beautiful in a deep purple dress and matching jacket. She took his breath away.

Next to Abby sat her father, Carlos. Jace was glad father and daughter had had time to get to know each other. The three days spent at the ranch had been healing for them all. Jace's body had recovered enough as to not be as painful from the beating he'd received, though his mother had insisted on having a doctor come out to confirm the injuries were mending.

It had done Jace's heart good to see his mother and father spend so much time together. Abby had joined his mom, teaching the teenagers the lost art of how to balance a checkbook, citing learning how to manage money was a necessary life skill. His admiration and respect for Abby grew each moment they were together.

For Jace, spending more time with Abby had been an unexpected blessing. When she wasn't at the camp helping his mom, they continued the riding lessons with him firmly on the ground, per doctor's order, while Abby became more comfortable sitting in the saddle. She'd become adept at handling her mount.

At night, they'd all sit around the firepit, singing and talking. Abby made a mean s'more. The idyllic moments were cemented in his brain, but he couldn't forget a powerful cartel lurked outside the ranch perimeter. The cartel undoubtedly waited for a moment to strike.

A moment like today.

His nerves were stretched taut. The marshals service fully expected the cartel to attack the courthouse. It seemed the logical conclusion. With testimony from Carlos, Abby and Jace, there was no question an indictment would be handed down and a warrant issued for the arrests of Tomas Garcia, Marco Garcia and the many cartel members they'd been able to identify.

Extra guards were in place, and several marshals had donned civilian clothes in anticipation of the Garcia Cartel attempting to stop today's proceedings. They also anticipated arresting the suspected mole within the marshals service, Gavin's longtime administrative assistant, Regina.

Seraphina hadn't found any unusual money transfers in Regina's main checking account. However, she did discover Regina had several accounts in various banks throughout the state of Texas with the bare minimum balance. Odd, but not illegal. Then Sera learned Regina's home had been paid for in cash. A red flag, because there was no indication of accumulated earnings to make the purchase.

With more digging, they'd discovered Regina had safe-deposit boxes in each of the banks. None of this was proof of wrongdoing. Though it was suspicious enough for the marshals service to request a search warrant from the attorney general.

Jace could tell his father was broken up over the prospect of Regina being a traitor. Yet his dad had summoned Regina to the courthouse on the pretext of needing some documents regarding the Garcia Cartel case. Would she show up? If she was privy to an impending attack, she'd remain at headquarters.

Within a half hour, Regina stepped into the courthouse and approached with a briefcase in hand, throwing doubt on the suspicion she was involved with the cartel. Judging from the relief on his father's face, Gavin was having the same doubts.

The trill of Regina's ringtone echoed off the marble floors. All eyes turned to her as she dug her cell phone from her purse. Her face paled as she regarded the phone, and she moved down the hall, away from where Gavin waited in front of the grand jury room, to speak to the caller.

Jace strained to catch Regina's side of the conversation and was surprised to realize she spoke in perfect Spanish. She furtively glanced over her shoulder at Gavin and then at where Abby and Carlos sat. Regina's agitation was clear as she rapidly told the person on the other line *no* repeatedly.

Finally, she turned to face them, the phone in her hand and tears in her eyes. She walked toward Jace.

"Regina?" Gavin said, intercepting her.

She shook her head. "I'm so sorry. This call is for Miss Frost."

Abby rose, her brow furrowed with confusion. "Me?"

Jace was at her side within seconds. He

leaned in close and whispered in Abby's ear, "Put it on Speaker."

Abby nodded, taking the phone from Regina and pushing the speaker button. "This is Abigail Frost."

"Did you really think you would get away with this?"

The hard voice on the other end of the line pierced through Jace's composure. Marco. Hands fisting at his sides, Jace held himself still, his gaze meeting his father's.

"Who is this?" Abby demanded.

"You and your father will not say a word, or your cousin and her daughter will disappear."

Abby gasped. "Don't you dare hurt them!"

"If you don't walk out of the courthouse right now, their deaths will be on your head."

Jace grabbed the phone from Abby. "Marco, are you too afraid to show your face and give your threats in person?"

"Deputy Marshal Armstrong," Marco mocked. "Your ladylove saved you once, but if we ever do meet again, I won't be soft on you."

Soft? Was Marco's idea of being soft the vicious beating he'd meted out? Jace refused to put any credence in what Marco may or may not do. The man was obviously scared. Good.

Jace needed to focus on protecting Abby. This ordeal was almost over, and his assignment would be done. He had to make it possible for her to go back to her life. The only way to ensure her safety was by arresting Tomas and Marco. Without them, the cartel would flounder and die. A snake without its head.

"Even if Abby and her father do not testify, I will," Jace said, aware of Abby's startled stare.

"I would expect nothing less from you, Deputy, but believe me when I tell you, you will regret it. It's really a nice thing your mother does there at her camp."

Icy rage filled Jace's veins, followed swiftly by terror. The ranch was on the cartel's radar. Jace locked eyes with Regina. The regret and remorse in her expression only made him more furious. She'd betrayed the marshals service. She'd betrayed Gavin and the whole family. But why?

"I'm going to take you down, Marco, and you won't see me coming." Jace hung up the phone.

"Jace!" Abby grabbed his arm. "He's going to hurt Inez and her daughter. We have to do something."

Gavin stepped forward, motioning for officers to take Regina into custody. "What did you do?"

"Lawyer," she said with a grimace.

Jace passed the phone to Brian. "See if you can trace the call."

"On it." Brian hustled away.

Carlos put an arm around Abby. "We can't give in to the cartel. It will never stop."

"But Inez and Paulina! They are your family, too."

"The best thing you can do for your cousin and niece," Gavin said, "is to testify so we can get the indictment. Then we can take Marco into custody."

"He's right," Jace said, though he hated the circumstances and wished with all his might the situation were different. "We can't make a move on the cartel till we have an indictment. We won't get an indictment unless we all testify. I will testify, but we need the strength of you two, as well."

"I can't. Not if it means Inez's and Paulina's deaths. And your mother's in danger, too!" Abby's eyes welled with tears.

Jace took her hands in his and whispered in her ear. "Remember, there is one who will guard Inez and her daughter with his life. My dad will protect my mom."

Jace didn't want to reveal Miguel's betrayal of the cartel for the woman he loved. He didn't know how many other loyal people the cartel had in place and what ears were listening. Although Regina had two armed officers at her side, she wasn't far enough away not to hear. There was no guarantee she wouldn't find a way to pass on a message to the Garcias.

"We have to trust he won't let anything happen to her and Paulina. Or my mom." Jace squeezed Abby's hands. "And we need to pray to God we will be successful taking the cartel down."

Abby stared into his eyes for the longest time, and he realized there was no guarding his heart from her. She was everything to him. Her hurt was like a physical blow. His own happiness was tied to hers. His heart beat for her.

He loved her.

The realization nearly knocked him to his knees.

He shoved the emotion to the side. Emotion had no place in his life. He couldn't function if sentiment interfered. He had to keep his judgment clear. Stay focused on the task at hand. "Trust me. This is the right decision."

She seemed to gather her composure. "You're right," she said. "I'll testify." She turned to her father, her gaze questioning.

Carlos nodded. "I will, too. This has to end."

Gavin put his hand on Jace's shoulder. "I'm going to take Regina to an interrogation room and find out why she's done this."

"What about Mom?"

"Don't worry, son. I have safety measures in place. Everyone at the ranch will be well protected, but I'll alert Victoria. She'll understand what to do."

Jace had no doubt his mom's safety was his father's biggest priority and that she and the campers would be safe.

The door to the grand jury room opened, and a man stepped out. "Abigail Frost."

Jace pulled her in for a hug. "You've got this."

She hung on to him for a moment. "Promise me you will not make a move on the Garcia Cartel without me. I want to be there when you take them down. I need to see for myself that Inez and Paulina are safe."

Jace didn't want to promise such a thing. But the stubborn set of her chin and the hard gleam in her eyes made it clear Abby would not walk into the grand jury room and testify without his assurance. "I promise."

Secure in the knowledge Jace would not break the pledge he'd made her, Abby walked into the grand jury room. She told them everything she could about the cartel, about their attempts to kidnap her and how she'd been held hostage at the compound. The proceedings were relatively painless, and she breathed a relieved sigh to have it behind her when she walked out a half hour later.

Carlos and Jace gave their testimonies regarding the cartel and the events leading them to this point. They didn't have to wait long before an indictment was handed over to the district attorney, who then sent a message to the marshals service, granting warrants for the arrest of Tomas Garcia, Marco Garcia and everyone within the Garcia employ, as well as seizure of all assets.

It was a mad scramble of activity as they

prepared to execute the warrants. Jace, Gavin, Carlos and Abby were escorted by police to the airport, where they boarded a JPATS plane bound for Laredo. More police escorted them to the Laredo marshals' headquarters.

At Jace's insistence, Abby put on a Kevlar vest over her dress suit. Likewise, her father slipped one on over his dress shirt under his jacket.

Jace had changed from his suit into tactical gear, a flak vest and utility belt. He'd slung an automatic rifle across his chest. The whole effect made Abby shudder with alarm.

"It's not too late," Jace told her, apparently misinterpreting her upset. "You can stay here. I'll inform you the moment we have them in custody."

"You promised," she reminded him. "I can handle this."

He nodded, though she could tell he wasn't happy about accommodating her. But she wasn't happy about the situation, either. Her cousin had risked her life to ensure Abby and Jace escaped the compound. The least Abby could do was be here when it all went down, to be a friendly face for Inez and her daughter after they were liberated.

Gavin joined them. "It's time. Abby and Carlos, you'll ride with Jace and me."

A long line of black SUVs waited along the back side of the building. Gavin hopped into the second-to-last SUV. Abby noted Brian and Sera getting into the first vehicle. Other agents she hadn't been introduced to climbed into the rest of them.

A flutter of anxiety hit Abby as she slid into the back and shut the door. Last time she'd been in an SUV like this, the cartel had disabled it. She leaned forward. "What if we don't make it there?"

Jace gave her a reassuring smile. "We've taken precautions."

She had to be content with his certainty. The drive to the compound was suffused with tension.

Her curiosity prompted her to ask, "Gavin,

did you discover why Regina was helping the Garcias?"

"After her lawyer showed up, she finally confessed she is related to the Garcias. She's a fourth cousin and was strategically placed in the Justice Department," Gavin answered. "We had no idea."

"There are probably others," Jace predicted.

"Indeed," Gavin replied.

Abby hated to contemplate how far and wide the cartel's reach was, and what law enforcement agencies the Garcias had infiltrated. She hoped the corruption would end once they had the Garcias in custody and they were stripped of their power and their resources. But she wasn't that naive. Corruption could be perpetrated from behind bars.

Abby gasped as Brian's SUV did not stop at the entrance but rammed through the gate. Gunfire erupted, the loud sound jarring and intense.

Abby squawked and ducked down, putting her hands over her head. Gavin pulled the SUV off to the shoulder, remaining outside the compound entrance.

"We're not going in?" Jace asked his father.

"Our job is to protect the witnesses."

Abby could sense Jace itched to get in on the fight. But she had to admit she was grateful both men stayed put.

The battle for control over the compound lasted far longer than Abby would've liked. Police and sheriff's departments from all over the state joined them. It seemed the cartel had made many enemies within law enforcement.

Finally, there was silence.

Static coming across the car's radio system preceded Brian's voice. "We have control of the compound. Tomas Garcia's in custody. Marco Garcia is nowhere to be found."

Jace pounded his fist on the dashboard.

"The tunnel?" Abby asked.

Shaking his head, Jace said, "We secured the other end. I suppose Marco could be down in the tunnel, but it's doubtful. He probably left here the moment he hung up the phone after threatening you."

"And left his father to be captured," Carlos said. "Sounds like Marco."

Gavin popped open his door. "I'll be right back."

Abby put her hand on Jace's shoulder. "I'm sorry you had to stay here with us."

For a moment, he didn't move. Then he twisted in his seat and took her hand. He lifted her knuckles to his lips. "You are my priority."

Carlos cleared his throat. "I'll step out."

Jace released Abby and opened his door. "We all should."

As soon as Abby climbed from the vehicle, she couldn't stop herself from flinging her arms around Jace's waist and hugging him tightly. "It's over."

He lifted her face to his. "Not yet. It won't be over until I hunt down Marco Garcia."

Her stomach took a nosedive. "But can't someone else go after him?"

A commotion drew their attention. Miguel, Inez and eleven-year-old Paulina were being escorted out of the compound entrance by Brian and Sera.

With a small cry of joy, Abby left Jace's arms to run to Inez and give her a hug. "I was so worried about you."

Inez held her tightly. "Funny. I was worried about *you*."

Abby introduced Carlos.

"I'm sorry it's taken these circumstances to meet you, Uncle," Inez said.

"Agreed. Your mother?" Carlos asked.

"They've taken her into custody."

Carlos turned to Jace. "May I talk to my sister?"

"I'll escort you," Brian said.

Her father and Brian walked back through the compound gates.

Abby turned to Miguel, who'd remained silently observing. "Thank you for everything."

He put his arm around Inez. "It was my pleasure."

"We need to go." Sera led the three to a waiting vehicle.

"Where are they going?" Abby asked Jace.

"To a safe place until they can give their statements, and then, hopefully, they will enter into WITSEC," Jace replied. "Miguel betrayed his cartel brothers. There are some members we haven't caught yet. Miguel will have a price on his head."

Abby shivered at the implication their lives would be in danger from now on. "What about Carlos?"

"Once Marco is arrested and put behind bars, your father can enter WITSEC as well, if he chooses, but I have a feeling he's done hiding."

Carlos deserved to live without the fear of being silenced. "And me?"

Jace cupped her cheek. "You go back to your life. I will make sure you're guarded twenty-four-seven until I find Marco. Once he is in custody and behind bars, you can resume your life without worry. I will make sure the cartel never hurts anyone again."

As great as his pronouncement sounded, she longed for the day when fear wasn't a living entity breathing down her neck. "That's all well and good, and I'm grateful. But, Jace, what about you and me?"

He dropped his hand from her face and stepped back. "There is no 'you and me' beyond today."

Each word battered at her heart. He didn't really believe there was no hope for them, did he? She stepped forward, closing the distance he'd put between them. She couldn't accept his words. Wouldn't accept his words. He'd taught her to be strong and to fight for what she wanted. He'd called her brave and courageous. She wanted to live up to his expectations. "Jace, I love you."

He shook his head and stepped back again. "Please, don't say that. I can't… I can't put you and a potential family through what my mother and I went through."

Little knives of anguish sliced into her.

The wounds throbbed. Her old self would have retreated, would have put up walls to keep out the heartache, but she was a different woman because of this man. She wasn't going to give in to self-protection to avoid what needed to be said. Once again, she closed the distance, this time grabbing ahold of him to keep him in place. Though she'd anticipated his resistance, she hadn't realized how much his unwillingness to give them a chance would hurt.

"Your parents protected you as best they could. They thought keeping you in the dark was the right thing to do." Her heart ached with desperation to make Jace understand they could have a different, brighter future together. "We can do things differently. While we can adopt your mother and father's pact of constant communication morning and night, we can also make a pact we will never keep our children in the dark."

She couldn't believe she was bringing children into this scenario when she didn't even know what was in his heart. Yet the agony on his face and the tenderness in his eyes made her confident he loved her but was too afraid to admit it. "Please, don't let fear come between us."

He framed her face with his big, strong calloused hands. "You undo me."

He claimed her mouth in a kiss. Sensation rocketed through her. She clung to him, hoping and praying with everything in her that his kiss was a declaration of his love. She needed him in her life. He was the missing part of her. Having finally found him, she couldn't imagine a future without him.

When he broke away, he peeled her hands from his flak vest and took two steps back. "I'm sorry."

He turned and motioned for a police officer to stand guard over her before striding away, leaving her with a bleeding heart.

SIXTEEN

Jace brought his rented sedan to a halt in the parking lot of a nondescript motel on the outskirts of San Diego. The two-story, open-balcony building sat opposite one of the many marinas dotting the shoreline. Three months of chasing leads on Marco across the country had left Jace exhausted, exasperated and furious. Every false tip was a strike against the marshals service, against Jace. Marco had proved to be crafty, moving stealthily from one location to another, uncatchable. So far.

Beneath his breath, Jace sent up a prayer. God willing, today would be the day they finally took the man down. Beside him, his father stirred, having dozed on the drive from the airport. They were both running on fumes and coffee. Gripping the steering wheel, Jace searched their surroundings for any sign of Marco.

Jace couldn't let the man remain free, not when there was a chance Marco would seek revenge against Abby, Carlos or the Armstrongs for all he had lost.

Since the takedown at the compound, Tomas Garcia and everyone else law enforcement had rounded up were sitting in jail awaiting trial. Extensive vetting of all the marshal employees was in process. Miguel, Inez and her daughter were safely tucked away in an undisclosed location, preparing to give their testimony before a jury.

Carlos was also squirreled away in a safe house known only by his handler, awaiting his moment in court. His testimony would have to wait until they had Marco in custody.

And then there was Abby.

She was being protected by both Sera and Brian. Sera had moved into the apartment across the hall from Abby. The same one Jace had occupied during his short stay in Camas. Brian was staying at the home of Mrs. Frost and Nancy. During the day, the two women were guarded by the Camas police while both Brian and Sera were at the bank branch throughout Abby's workday to keep her safe.

Jace received regular updates on Abby and her well-being, but it wasn't enough. He missed her desperately. He hated being separated from her. He thought the sensation of loneliness and desperation to be with her would go away in time, but so far, the need had only increased. The sensation of suffocating every second he was without her in his life had become overwhelming. He never should have walked away from her. He had let his fear take over.

Shame was a monkey on his back. Abby would never let fear or uncertainty stop her. She'd shown him as much from the moment he'd met her. He'd been an idiot not to recognize her strength. And even more so to deny his love for her. He was denying his own heart.

"When we find Marco and put him behind bars, I'm going to put in for a transfer to the Pacific Northwest office," he said.

His father jammed his cowboy hat on his head and gave a sage nod. "It's about time you came to the right conclusion."

Jace drew back. "What do you mean?"

Gavin's gaze was direct and filled with affection. "Your mother and I have been praying you would realize what a great match you and Abby would make."

Warmth spread through Jace's heart. He and his dad had had numerous conversations over the past three months as they traveled around the country searching for Marco. Jace had come to terms with the way he'd been raised, especially after his dad talked about his own father, who'd been killed in the line of duty. Jace understood now, and as Abby had said, they could make different choices for their lives, for their children's lives. Assuming she still loved him.

The thought she might have changed her mind sliced a stinging wound through his midsection.

His father popped open the door of the sedan. Jace reached back for his own hat and put it on his head. It was time to focus.

There would be time to tell Abby he was ready to let down the walls around his heart. To tell her he loved her and wanted to spend his life with her. But first, Marco.

The sea breeze coming off the Pacific Ocean tasted of salt. In the distance, the waves lapping against the coastline played the earth's anthem.

Jace and his father headed into the reception area and approached the counter. The female clerk glanced up from a popular celebrity magazine and smiled. "How can I help you?"

Jace showed the woman his badge, as did his father. Then Jace held up Marco's photo to the desk clerk. "Is this man staying in this motel?"

The woman squinted at the photo.

"Maybe." She eyed Jace and Gavin. "What has he done?"

"Sorry, classified," Gavin retorted. "We need his room number."

She lifted her eyebrows. "Do you have a warrant?"

"We can get one," Gavin said. "But it will take time. The man is a wanted fugitive. His room number. Please."

The woman bobbed her head, and her fingers flew over the keyboard of her computer. "Mr. Smith is in room two-twenty-eight."

"Do you know if he's currently in his room?"

"I do not."

Gavin held out his hand. "A key?"

The woman sighed, made an electronic key and handed the card over to Gavin.

They took the outside staircase. Jace was glad the room faced the back of the property, so there was less chance of alerting Marco to their presence. As they approached the door to 228, it opened, and a housekeeping cart was wheeled out by a woman wearing a uniform.

Frustration bunched Jace's muscles, squeezing tightly and sending a pounding rush through his brain. He doubted Marco was inside the room. Hopefully, he was just out while the room was being cleaned, but Jace wasn't going to hold his breath.

Gavin showed his badge to the woman. "Is the guest inside?"

She shook her head. "Nope. He left."

"What do you mean he left?" Jace bit out.

"Packed up and skedaddled. I don't know when."

Jace clenched his jaw and was surprised he didn't crack a tooth. Another dead end.

Gavin held up his phone with the picture of Marco on it. "Was this the man staying in this room?"

The housekeeper tilted her head and studied the photo. "Yes. Only he shaved all the hair off."

"Do you mean he no longer has a beard and mustache?" Gavin asked.

She nodded. "No mustache, beard or hair on his head."

A new lead, at least. Though having missed Marco made Jace's blood pressure boil. "Do you mind if we poke around the room?"

The woman shrugged and pushed the cart to the next room. Jace hesitated and then asked the woman, "Did you empty his trash bins?"

"Of course."

"I need them."

She reached into a big garbage container and picked up the tied-off plastic bag on top. "This was everything in his room."

Jace took the bag and entered the hotel room. Everything was neat and tidy. There was nothing in the drawers, closet or under the bed.

After slipping on thin protective gloves, Jace ripped open the plastic bag and dumped the contents on the floor. He sifted through fast-food containers and found a wadded-up piece of paper. He smoothed it out on the desk. There was a series of four numbers followed by a space and then a number and a letter. "What do you make of these?"

His father peered over his shoulder. "Bank account numbers?"

Jace shook his head. "Part of an address?" He pulled an evidence baggie from his pocket and stuck the paper inside.

They left the room, and as they passed the housekeeper, Jace said, "Sorry, I made a mess." He took out his wallet and handed her a twenty-dollar bill.

She took the money with a smile. "Have a good day."

When they reached the ground floor, his father headed back toward the sedan, but before he followed, Jace was struck by an idea. He pivoted and entered the reception area again. He held up the piece of paper he'd found in Marco's garbage for the clerk to view. "Any idea what these might be?"

The woman stared at the paper for a moment and then nodded. "Flight number and seat number."

Of course. Jace's heart thudded, and his pulse raced. Marco was taking a flight somewhere. They needed to know where he was heading and if they could intercept the flight. "Any chance Mr. Smith used the business center?"

"I have no idea. It's on the lower floor. He wouldn't have come by here to get to it unless he wanted to take the elevator."

Gavin rejoined Jace. "What's up?"

"This could be a flight and seat number." Jace strode to the staircase leading to the basement level. His father fell into step with him. "We should check the business center. Maybe Marco used their computer."

"Good idea."

Jace soaked up his father's approval as he shoved open the door to the business center. A man with a nameplate with the name Ken was busy boxing up packages behind the counter. Jace flashed his badge and showed the man Marco's photo. "Have you seen him?"

"Yes, he was here waiting as I opened this morning." Ken pointed to the nearest monitor and keyboard. "He sat there."

Gavin sat down in front of the computer. "Is there a way to search the browse history on this?"

"Not as far as I know. It's only for printing boarding passes," Ken said.

"Is there any way for you to tell us what airline he was flying?" Jace asked.

"Not from that computer, I can't." Ken came out from behind the counter and headed to the printer. "The guy in the photo was the only one who printed anything today. I'll hit Print again, and it should give us whatever he printed."

He pushed a button, and the machine whirred and spit out a piece of paper. It was a boarding pass for a popular airline. Jace's heart sank when he realized the flight had already landed in Portland,

Oregon. Dread filled his veins and terror made his hands shake. "He's going after Abby."

Abby sat at her desk inside the Pacific Northwest Savings and Loan, reading bank reports from the past six months, but her eyes kept glazing over as memories assaulted her. One would think after three months she'd be able to put the horrors of being a target of the Garcia Cartel and the heartbreak of having Jace walk away behind her, but the memories surfaced at odd times, and her heart ached.

There had been no word from Jace since that fateful day, though she was convinced Sera and Brian were in contact with him. However, both marshals told her it was better if she wasn't privy to what was going on. Had Jace asked them to keep her in the dark? Was he repeating the pattern he'd learned from his father? Or did he truly want nothing more to do with her?

Either way, she was heartsick she might

never see him again. She'd told him she loved him, and he'd walked away.

Which should have been enough for her to let go of him, but it wasn't. She wanted another chance to make him comprehend they could have a future together. If only he'd let her.

There was a knock at her office door. "Yes, Tina?"

"There's a customer who's demanding to see the branch manager." Tina shrugged. "Paul's on break getting coffee for everyone."

"I'll be right there." Abby stood, adjusted her skirt and walked out of the office. Her gaze met Sera, who sat at an added desk near the front entrance. They'd created a position for her as greeter until Marco was caught.

Abby wasn't sure what the marshal did sitting there all day, but she always seemed to be busy on the provided computer. Abby gestured with her head toward the row of tellers. Sera nodded and stood, picked up a stack of file folders and discreetly followed Abby.

Abby's lips twitched. Sera's billowy skirts and jackets with frilly blouses beneath made the tough-as-nails marshal a walking cliché of an old-fashioned librarian from some fifties sitcom. She'd even swept her hair up into a severe bun on the top of her head and wore cat-eye-shaped glasses.

It was certainly enough of a disguise to prevent anyone from identifying her as the female US marshal who had been a part of the takedown of the Garcia Cartel.

As Abby approached the row of tellers' windows, the customer in question left his place at the second-to-last window and headed toward her. His long legs ate up the distance.

The man had on a ball cap pulled low over a shaved head and bright blue tinted glasses. A baggy bomber jacket engulfed his thin frame. He had one hand buried in the jacket pocket. There was nothing particularly interesting about the man, yet

Abby couldn't stop the shiver prickling her skin.

She backed up a step as the man halted in front of her.

"Can I help you?" Abby said after an uncomfortable silence.

"Yes." The man closed the distance between them in a flash and grabbed ahold of her arm, his fingers biting into her skin. He leaned in close. "I have a gun aimed at your heart. If you want to live, if you want the people in this bank to live, you will leave with me."

Shock reverberated through Abby as the voice triggered a memory of the phone call she'd received in the courthouse the day she'd testified before the grand jury. Marco.

Frantic with fear, her gaze sought Sera, who stood only a couple of paces away.

Sera gave a subtle nod, her gaze intense.

Obviously, Sera understood what was happening and was telling her to cooperate. In a loud voice, Abby said, "I can help you with the ATM. Come outside and let me show you."

Marco squeezed her arm. "Clever girl," he said beneath his breath.

They headed for the exit and the guard manning the door. Abby met Brian's gaze. He acted casual as he pushed the door open for her. "Miss Frost. Watch your step."

Taken aback by the cryptic words, she said, "Thank you."

As she and Marco passed through the doorway, Abby interpreted Brian's words as a call to action. She brought the heel of her shoe down on Marco's foot as hard as she could. He howled and brought out a gun from the pocket of his jacket. Brian, still holding the door, swung it inward to crash against Marco's side.

Marco grunted but aimed the barrel of the gun at Abby.

Her breath stalled. Then she was yanked away from Marco at the same time someone in a US Marshals jacket and a cowboy hat tackled him, taking him down to the cement in front of the bank's double swinging doors. Jace?

Brian piled on, and Sera came blasting out the door with a gun drawn. More police officers and marshals materialized from around the bank and the parking lot.

The hands holding Abby gentled, and she turned to find herself standing next to Gavin Armstrong. Shock washed over her, followed quickly by relief. She sagged against him. "You're here?"

Her gaze jumped to the back of the US marshal at the bottom of the pile wrestling with Marco. She caught a glimpse of Jace's dear face as he and Marco grappled for control of the gun. Her lungs seized. She thought she might collapse with the jolt of fear mixed with joy at the sight of him.

The loud report of the gun going off echoed in her ears, momentarily disorienting her. Slowly, the pile of people trying to manhandle Marco into submission retreated, until only Marco lay on the ground. Blood seeped from the hole in his chest, his hand still wrapped around the weapon.

Jace stood, running his hands through his hair as Brain applied pressure to the awful wound.

Abby broke away from Gavin and rushed to Jace's side, then threw her arms around him. Pandemonium ensued as an ambulance arrived and the police officers and marshals vied for jurisdiction.

Abby drew Jace away from the chaos as Marco was loaded into the back of the ambulance, Brian climbing in behind him.

"How did you know Marco was here?" she asked.

"Our hard work paid off. I'm just glad we made it in time." Jace cupped her face. "Are you okay?"

"I am now that you're here." She nuzzled into his touch. "Please, tell me you're not going to leave me again?"

He rubbed the pad of his thumb over her bottom lip. "I've thought of nothing but getting back to you since the day I walked away. Can you forgive me?"

Joy burst in her heart. "Of course I can forgive you. I love you, Jace."

His expression filled with tenderness. "I've thought about what you said. You were right. We can make different decisions than my parents did. But honestly, after talking to my dad and realizing the scope of his own issues with having a father who was killed in the line of duty, I understand now why he protected me the way he did."

Were they on the same page with regard to their future? "So does this mean you could…? I mean, do you…?"

He smiled. The happiness in his eyes nearly made her weep. "I love you, Abby. If you will have me, I would love to marry you and spend my life with you. We will find the right balance together."

Delight swept over her, and she threw her arms around his neck. "Yes! A million times, yes. I can relocate to Texas."

He grinned. "I'll transfer to the Pacific Northwest."

She laughed. "It doesn't matter where we live, as long as we're together."

He pulled her closer for a kiss. As she gave herself over to his passionate embrace, she vowed she would never let him go, even though she realized she would have to trust Jace to God's care every day.

Jace lifted his head. "What do you say about a trip to Italy for our honeymoon?"

He'd remembered. Her heart melted, and adoring love filled her being. "Sounds fabulous."

Six months later...

"I now pronounce you husband and wife." The voice of the pastor of Abby's church rang loud and clear. "You may kiss the bride."

With joy, Abby met Jace halfway for a heart-melting, toe-curling kiss.

Cheers erupted throughout the sanctuary.

Giddy with happiness, Abby gathered the train of her beaded silk wedding dress with one hand and clung to Jace with the other as they turned to face the congregation.

Abby's heart was full as her gaze landed on her mother, whose arm was around Carlos's. With Marco dead and Tomas Garcia convicted of numerous crimes along with the majority of the cartel members, Carlos had decided to move to Camas and rekindle his relationship with Abby's mom.

Jace had taken a position at the Portland US Marshals Service office, and Abby had been given a promotion. She was now the manager of a small branch in a suburb of Portland. They'd bought a house they would move into as soon as they returned from their Italian honeymoon.

Lisa nudged Abby with the bouquet she held, offering it back to Abby. Lisa and Nancy were Abby's bridesmaids, stunning in matching rose-colored tea-length dresses, while Brian and Sera, both wearing black—Brian in a tux matching Jace's and Sera in a black formal A-line affair—stood up for Jace.

Brian clapped Jace on the back. "Let's get this party started."

With a laugh, Jace and Abby led the procession out of the church and into their new life.

*****

If you enjoyed this story, look for these other books by Terri Reed:

Christmas Protection Detail
Secret Sabotage

Dear Reader,

With the advent of DNA profiling being so readily available to the public, it's inevitable secrets could be uncovered, lives disrupted and mysteries solved. A search of the internet reveals multiple stories of people discovering relatives they never dreamed existed. Though my story is fictional, it is inspired by a dear friend's personal revelation of when she and her siblings took a DNA test. The effects rippled through two families. However, no cartel was involved. The Garcias were my "what-if" to catapult the plot down a dangerous path.

Abby isn't a real person, but her struggle to understand and come to terms with secrets and the past is certainly real enough. I tried to imagine how I would react to learning the man I had called father wasn't actually the man whose blood flowed through my veins. Adding on being targeted by a ruthless cartel made for a fast-paced story I hope you enjoyed.

Of course, Abby had to have the right man to protect her. At the time I was developing the characters, I was reading a series of books about cowboys. Who doesn't love cowboys? Jace struggled to open his heart due to anxiety about the effects his job would have on those he loved. Thankfully, Abby, his warrior queen, made him realize love can conquer fear, and together they could find a balance for a bright future.

If you would like to keep up with my new releases, sign up for my newsletter at www.terrireed.com.

May God bless you,
Terri